My Father the Horse Thief

My Father the Horse Thief

JERRY JERMAN

THE JOURNEYS OF JESSIE LAND

The Long Way Home
My Father the Horse Thief
Phantom of the Pueblo (July, 1995)
Danger at Outlaw Creek (July, 1995)

Cover design by Scott Rattray
Cover illustration by Michael Garland
Copyediting by Afton Rorvik, Liz Duckworth

Library of Congress Cataloging-in-Publication Data

Jerman, Jerry, 1949–
My father, the horse thief / by Jerry Jerman.
p. cm.—(The Journeys of Jessie Land)
Summary: The disappearance of a horse and Jessie's father sends Jessie on a search that takes her into danger.
ISBN 1-56476-347-1
[1. Missing persons—Fiction. 2. Christian life—Fiction. 3. Mystery and detective stories.] I. Title. II. Series: Jerman, Jerry, 1949– Journeys of Jessie Land.
PZ7.J54My 1995
[Fic]—dc20 94-32672
CIP
AC

---

1 2 3 4 5 6 7 8 9 10 Printing/Year 99 98 97 96 95

All characters and events portrayed in this book are fictitious. While Will Rogers and his horse Soapsuds did live on a ranch in Santa Monica in 1935, their appearance here is a creation of the author. Also, some liberties have been taken in describing the geography of both the ranch and Santa Monica.

To Lynn Kostoff, Vicki Grove,
and Larry Colbert
with affection and many thanks

Chapter 1

"Where'dja get that ugly bike?"

The boy's words stung. I stood outside Hopper's store that Friday morning in June, my homemade bicycle behind me. I felt my face grow red. The boy's mouth turned down like a bulldog's. He wore clean new clothes and his face and hands looked scrubbed. Beside him, his two younger brothers stared at me. I had no fear of them, but the tall boy's words and those three faces made me feel like some kind of vile bug.

When I didn't answer, the tall boy broke out, "What're you, a dirty *and* deaf Okie?"

That last word cut deep. I looked sharply at him. "Are you talking to me, you rude child?" I asked, my fingers straying to cover a patch on my overalls.

The little boys laughed and began singing, "Okie trash, Okie trash." I'd heard these taunts before. I tried to ignore them as best I could.

The bell on the door to Hopper's store tinkled, and a woman in a white frilly dress stepped out. She called, "Henry! Willis! Stephen! Come here! Stay away from that filthy girl."

I shuddered at her words. Tears sprang into my eyes. *Filthy!* I'd taken a bath just last night.

Anger quickly replaced my shame. Glaring at the woman, I declared, "I am no more filthy than these ill-bred sons of yours, ma'am, and they're in sore need of manners."

Her mouth gaped open as if amazed I had the wits to speak to her. "Mind your own manners!" she lashed back as she led the jeering boys off across the street. I turned my face away. There was no shame in crying, but I wouldn't let the likes of them see my tears.

My body shook with the unrightness of those boys' taunts. Why had they picked on me? I'd been minding my own business.

Trying to cheer myself, I concentrated on the bright red bike with shiny chrome fenders in the store window. Such a beauty it was. Then my eyes settled on the price tag. Twelve dollars. A lot of money in 1935 when folks were without work and going hungry. Times were tough even here in Santa Monica, California, where I now lived with Mama and Daddy. Not far from our apartment a whole camp of folks barely survived. Still, I longed for this new bike more than anything else in the world.

My eyes drifted from the beautiful two-wheeler in the window to the homemade bike beside me—the bike that had roused those dreadful boys to mock me.

Ever since we settled in Santa Monica a few weeks ago, I had begged Daddy for a bike. Finally, he gathered up an assortment of spare parts and made me one himself. He found lengths of pipe and scraps of chain. He even came upon an actual bicycle wheel somewhere, though just one. The rear wheel he fashioned from wood. Then he gave the whole thing a couple coats of white paint, and I had myself one humdinger of a bicycle.

For a week it had been my pride and joy. But now, remembering the insults of those boys and gazing at that new bicycle in Hopper's window, it didn't suit me anymore. I considered its shortcomings. Its heaviness made it hard to steer, and it had none of the sleekness of the red beauty on the other side of the glass.

Suddenly the front door of the store burst open, the bell tinkling. A well-dressed man with plastered-down blond hair and a moustache gazed at me with bright green eyes. He plunged his hands into his gray trouser pockets and jingled some coins. His large gold cufflinks and highly polished black shoes reflected the hot California sun.

A smile relaxed his mouth and his eyes crinkled. This was Mr. Lex Hopper himself, owner and proprietor. "Well, Jessie Land, got your eyes full again?" he asked. He meant the bicycle. I'd been by to admire it before.

Nodding, I replied, "It's the grandest bicycle I've ever seen anywhere."

He stooped beside my homemade bike and ran his hand over it. I felt my face flush. It always embarrassed me when people gave it too much attention. As with the boys, it usually meant they were about to make fun of it.

"Get much riding out of this contraption?" he asked.

"Oh, yes!" I exclaimed, relieved to point out its merits.

"I've ridden all over town. And all the back roads outside town too."

"But it's on the heavy side for you, I'd wager," he said. With two fingers he gave it a hoist, testing its weight. *"Whoa!* Goodness, how do you steer this thing?"

"It's a little hard," I admitted.

He stood up and plunged his hands back into his pockets. He must have had a heap of change in there from the racket it made as he jingled it.

Seeming to size me up, he said, "Maybe your father could buy you this one." He motioned toward the red beauty. "He's got himself a good job, working for Mr. Rogers."

Incredible as it seemed, for three weeks Daddy had been working for the famed Will Rogers, on Mr. Rogers' ranch just outside of town.

"I don't know," I began. "Daddy doesn't make a lot of money. And then there's Mama and me and—"

"You could put something down on the bike," Mr. Hopper explained. "Your father could pay it off gradually. I do that all the time for working folks."

What could I say? Of course, I would have loved to own that bicycle. More than anything. Maybe Daddy did have a dollar or two he could put down on it.

As I gave some thought to Mr. Hopper's words, a boy, younger than me, slipped up to the door of the store. He looked like he came from the migrant camp. He wore a ragged, dirty shirt, a dusty cap, shoes with holes, and a pair of trousers stitched together from flour sacks.

Mr. Hopper stopped him. "Just where do you think you're going?" he demanded.

The boy froze and studied the sidewalk in front of him. He whimpered, "M-m-mama said you might have some scissors."

"You have money for scissors, boy?"

The boy glanced up and opened a grimy fist. I saw two pennies there.

"All out of two-cent scissors," declared Mr. Hopper. "You'd best get home." When the boy didn't budge, the store owner insisted, *"Off with you—now!"*

The boy took off. My heart ached for him.

Turning back to me, Mr. Hopper complained, "That filthy child's stolen from my store twice already. Comes in acting like a customer, then he filches something when I turn away. Can't trust a single soul from that camp, you know?"

I nodded but immediately felt bad for it. My best friend, Leo Little Wolf, and his family lived in the camp. Leo was as honest as they come.

Giving me a brief smile, Mr. Hopper said, "You talk to your folks about that bike now. All right?" He didn't wait for me to answer but strode back into his store.

I climbed on my crude bicycle and pedaled away. The wooden wheel jolted me over stray rocks. My hands clenched the rough pipe that served as handlebars. When Daddy had put the bike together, I was so excited, so proud. Never in my twelve years had I owned a bicycle. But now I saw it like those awful boys did—as a piece of Okie junk.

On the way home I spied words scrawled on the side of a building. In bold and ugly letters they read:

OKIES GO HOME!

I shivered, knowing these words were aimed at me and Mama and Daddy. Why must folks be so hateful?

I rode past men and women lined up for jobs in the stores and the canneries. They stared at the ground, their hands dug deep into their pockets. I couldn't bear to look at them and I pedaled hard. I thought of the red bicycle. Could it be that Mama and Daddy might buy it for me? Daddy *did* have a good job. Maybe. . . .

I slowed at the squatty, pale yellow apartment building where we lived. Big chunks of stucco crumbled at the corners. I hopped off my bike and wheeled it around to the back. There in the weeds sat our car, an Essex. The black, boxy vehicle was missing its fenders and running board on one side. The car's engine had conked out a few days ago. To get to work Daddy hiked the three miles to Mr. Rogers' ranch. Come Sunday, after church, he planned to get the vehicle running again.

I stood beside the Essex gazing at my reflection in the window glass. I saw a clean but none too neat girl with a dimpled chin and brown eyes and bright red hair cut like a boy's, wearing patched overalls, pushing a bicycle assembled from scrap parts. A pretty sorry picture, I had to admit. The scaly apartment building behind me didn't help.

At once I felt ashamed. I looked just like an Okie—someone who came to California from Oklahoma or Missouri or Arkansas or Texas or Kansas. It didn't matter to folks around here. We were all Okies to them. All no-accounts.

Then I thought, *I may look like trash, but Mama and Daddy and me—we aren't no-accounts!*

Leaning my bike against our car, I climbed into the front seat and gripped the wheel. I'd done some driving back in Oklahoma on our tenant farm. All farm kids did. Daddy said I had a natural instinct for handling the wheel.

"Well," I told myself, pretending to drive, "you might have come here from Oklahoma by way of Kansas, but that doesn't make you worthless."

I recalled these past five incredible weeks. Crossing half the country to get here and then Daddy getting a job with Will Rogers, the moving picture star! A lady pilot I knew named Hazel Womack, who'd helped me get to California, was a good friend of Mr. Rogers. She told him all about me and my family and he took us in. Treated us just like kin. He helped us find an apartment in town and gave Daddy a job. Mr. Rogers had learned for himself what a reliable and good worker George Land was, especially with the horses.

My mind then strayed to that new bike in Hopper's store. Folks would treat me differently if I came riding down the street on a thing like that. Imagine their faces.

Aloud, I said, "They'd say, 'Now there goes a right smart young lady. Not at all like those dirty Okies. You can tell by her bicycle and the way she sits on it.' "

Suddenly, I bolted upright. *The bike!* It would be just the thing to make folks respect me. Surely I could get Mama and Daddy to see that. I just had to have that bike!

Leaping out of our old car, I rushed into the apartment building, raced down the hall, and burst open our door.

"Mama!" I cried.

I stopped short. Mama sat slumped on the threadbare gray couch. Tears glistened in her brown eyes. Her pale hands wrung a frayed handkerchief.

Stepping in, I saw Frank Dubois, the foreman from Will Rogers' ranch. A tall, lanky man with a red face and a red bandanna tied around his neck, he slouched beside the sofa. He frowned and clenched a tan hat that looked like a herd of horses had tromped on it.

All thought of the new bike flew from my mind.

"Mama!" I cried, running to her. "What's wrong?"

Her face paled as she gazed at me. She wiped her eyes with the handkerchief.

"What's wrong?" I repeated. I felt tears come to my own eyes and I didn't even know the reason.

She reached out and tugged me into her arms. With a soft voice she said, "It's your daddy. He's. . . ."

I gasped, feeling a horrible chill course through me.

Behind me Frank Dubois cleared his throat. I turned to look at him.

"What is it, Frank?" I asked. "What's happened?"

His red face reddened, but he said nothing.

"We don't know where he is, honey," Mama said.

"Your daddy's disappeared."

Her words struck at me like fists. *Disappeared!* How could he? Daddy went to work yesterday at Mr. Rogers' ranch. He told Mama he'd be working late getting the place spruced up for the Rogers family, who were due back Sunday. He planned to stay the night at the ranch. This morning, Mama would be fixing up something for him to eat, and we'd take it out to him.

I rushed to explain, "He's at the ranch—"

"He ain't at the ranch," Frank blurted out. "Leastwise he wasn't there when I drove up this morning."

Something in their voices told me there was more to this than Daddy disappearing. As horrible as it might be, I had to know all of it.

"What is it, Mama?" I said. "Tell me everything."

She reached out and clutched me, then held my face between her cool thin hands. "Jessie—" she began.

"It's not just your father," the foreman interrupted. His face seemed suddenly to harden. "Mr. Rogers' favorite horse, Soapsuds, is gone too. Seems your father . . . well, he stole him."

Chapter 2

My father a horse thief? No! It couldn't be. Suddenly I felt like all my insides had been shaken out, like I was just a husk of a girl named Jessie Land and if Frank sneezed I'd be blown apart.

The words *horse thief* kept repeating in my head. Mama dabbed at her eyes, and Frank looked from her to me, all the time edging toward the door. He acted as if he couldn't wait to get out of our place.

"Daddy couldn't have stolen Mr. Rogers' horse," I declared finally.

Frank crushed his hat even more and said, "Why not?"

" 'Cause he's no horse thief," I said flatly, realizing it wasn't much in the way of proof. "He was thankful for the job Mr. Rogers gave him. Besides, he wouldn't steal anything from anyone."

Frank planted his hat on his head. It didn't look any better up there than it did squashed between his hands. He made a motion to go.

Mama sprang to her feet. Her eyes pleading, she said, "Frank, Jessie's right. My land, George wouldn't take what isn't his. He's a Christian man. He lives by his beliefs."

"Look, Marian," Frank said, his gray eyes on both of us. "I liked George the minute I met him."

Frank's on our side! I thought with relief. But then his jaw jutted out. That hard look returned to his eyes.

He continued, "But I've seen all sorts of men in this here Depression. You just can't tell what's in a man's heart no more. Besides, if he didn't steal the horse, why'd he disappear? Answer me that. Why'd he disappear?"

We didn't have an answer for that.

Frank went to the door. "One more thing," he said. He swung around and faced us. "Mr. Rogers gave me money to pay the help. Today's payday. But I don't think he'd want me paying it to you if George stole his horse."

What? It was a spiteful thing to say.

"Daddy's no horse thief," I shot back. "You're just jealous of him because Mr. Rogers likes him so much."

Frank's face reddened to the color of his bandanna. "That's a lie," he spat.

"It's not," I said.

Mama stepped between us. "My land, Frank, we need that money. George worked hard all week for it. He earned every penny of it."

"You'll have to take that up with Mr. Rogers," he said. "I've got troubles of my own, what with a wolf prowling around the ranch and a cabin Mr. Rogers wants built. And now I gotta see the sheriff about this sorry business."

He left without closing the door behind him. I listened to his boots stomping down the plank floor of the hallway.

When the sound faded, I turned to Mama. My head

throbbed with the awful things Frank had said.

Choking back a sob, I whispered, "Mama, what're we gonna do?"

She took me in her arms and held me tight. I let the tears go. They streamed down my cheeks and soaked into her faded, cotton dress. The whole time she whispered in my ear, her own voice full of sadness, "It'll be OK, Jessie. You'll see. It'll be OK."

After a while she pulled back and looked at me. I saw myself reflected in her face: the same fair complexion, the same bright, red hair, the same brown eyes, the same tears in those eyes. Mama wiped her face and clutched the handkerchief in her fist. Determination burned in her eyes.

"We both know your father's innocent and that he's likely in danger right now," she said. "We can't do some things, Jessie, but we can pray for his safety and for God to take care of him."

We did just that, on our knees beside the couch.

After we prayed, Mama stood up and declared, "The rent's due today and I haven't any money at all. Your father had a few dollars to buy parts for the car. But we need money right away."

I remembered the bicycle in Mr. Hopper's window, then felt guilty for my selfish thought.

Mama's voice grew tense. "Your father and I lived in a Hooverville when we first got to California." I'd seen plenty of Hoovervilles in California, migrant camps where a lot of sad, unemployed people lived without much hope.

"It was a miserable, filthy life we lived then and I'll not do it again. I'll pack us up and move us back to Liberal to live with my sister before I let that happen."

The thought of returning to Liberal, Kansas shook me. Just weeks ago I'd run away from Aunt Edna and her family. I'd been left with them while Mama and Daddy went on to look for work in California. They'd promised to send for me after six months, but six months passed and still I waited. And while I waited, Aunt Edna had chopped off my long hair because it was too "inconvenient." She'd also given me a good whacking most every day. Finally, I just took off on my own. With God's help and the aid of a couple of guardian angels, I found my parents. That migrant camp might be horrible, but I could never go back to that mean Aunt Edna. Never.

"I can find a job, Mama," I offered. "At a cannery. They must have loads of jobs."

She smiled slightly. "They've also got loads of people wanting jobs. I'd best see about it myself. Folks don't like to give jobs to children when adults are sore in need."

"But I'm twelve years old."

Mama touched my cheek with her fingertips. "Honey, your job is to be here. Stay close to home and wait for news of your father."

She started getting ready to go out.

I sat on the couch and thought about Daddy and Soapsuds. I knew Daddy had nothing to do with taking the horse. So why would he disappear too? Why?

He loved being around the horses on the ranch, especially Soapsuds because Mr. Rogers had taught him all sorts of peculiar tricks.

When we had lived on the tenant farm in southeastern Oklahoma, we had an old plow horse. Huey. A good horse but nothing like Mr. Rogers' flaky roan. Daddy once told me one of his first jobs as a young man had been tending horses on a ranch in Texas. He said he loved the smell and excitement of those animals. I guess that was one reason Mr. Rogers hired Daddy. They both loved horses.

But why would Daddy disappear with Soapsuds?

Mama had changed to a pretty but patched blue dress.

"Try to stay around the apartment," she advised me. "In case there's some word about your father."

"Yes, ma'am."

"Lord willing, I'll be back with a job."

As soon as she went out, I poked around the apartment for a time. There had to be something I could do to find Daddy. Frank had gone to the sheriff already. No need to head that way. I decided to ask my friend Leo Little Wolf to help me. Being an Indian, he'd probably be pretty good at tracking someone's whereabouts.

As I closed the door behind me, Mama's words came back to me. She had said "*try* to stay around the apartment." But to me, trying to stay around the apartment and actually staying around it were two different things.

Outside I picked up my bicycle and headed for the rough road leading to the camp on the edge of town. A lot of migrant workers lived in the San Joaquin Valley where there were crops to pick. Mama and Daddy had tried that, but they didn't like moving around from farm to farm. Like me, they wanted a place to settle down—a real home. A lot of other folks felt the same. They wanted to live in town but couldn't afford to rent an apartment or a motor court room. So they settled in the migrant camp till they found work.

During the day most of the men from the camp hunted for jobs. The women cooked in large, black pots hung over fires and tended the children. Half-dressed kids with dirty faces stared at folks passing by on the road. Some of them cried from hunger or weariness, and all of them looked plumb wore out. It was a sight to behold. It almost made me feel ashamed for ever wanting anything.

I found Leo exactly where I expected to. He stood in an open place twirling a rope. As usual, he chomped a wad of gum and talked to himself. He told me once he lived in the camp with his family, though I'd never seen a one of them.

"Yippie-i-o, ladies and gents, children and pets," he sang out. "Feast your eyes on this. I'll now perform for you the incredible lasso dance!"

I laid my bike on the ground and raced over to him.

"Leo, something terrible's happened," I yelled.

My friend waved to shut me up. He made a big loop and began spinning it over the ground. Then he hopped in and out of it. He'd picked up this skill from Mr. Rogers himself, who once or twice gave him a job clearing brush on his ranch, which was where Leo and I first met. Mr. Rogers was the best rope twirler in the world. He'd even given me a couple of lasso lessons.

"Leo, stop!" I cried. "I've *got* to talk to you."

He must have heard the fear in my voice because he dropped the rope and came over to me.

We were the same age, but Leo seemed younger, maybe because the top of his head only came to my chin. His long, black, unruly hair stuck out all over the place. He didn't care one whit for hairbrushes. His mouth looked tiny on his pudgy face. With short, stubby fingers he picked at some stray pieces of grass on his shirt. He was a Northern Cheyenne Indian and my best friend in California. He turned his dark eyes on me.

"Leo, Daddy's disappeared," I told him.

His face didn't change a bit as I reported this horrible fact. He didn't ask a question, didn't even seem alarmed.

"Did you hear me?" I asked, grabbing his arm. "It's Daddy—he's just *gone!*"

"Yep," he said.

"And Soapsuds—he's missing too!"

"Yep."

"And Frank thinks Daddy stole him."

"Yep. I know that too."

I stared wide-eyed at him. "You *know?*"

Nodding, he said, "Yep. I reckoned you'd come runnin' up here soon's you found out."

"But how'd you know?" I asked him.

"Gal, when an Okie's in trouble around here, the news spreads like wildfire," he declared, his hands on his hips. "And I heard somethin' else. There're some men who want to go after your pa with a rope and string him up."

Chapter 3

"String him up!" I cried. I couldn't believe Leo. "But why?"

"Will Rogers's 'bout as popular as they come 'round here, gal," my friend explained as he chomped the wad of gum in his mouth. He squinted the way Mr. Rogers sometimes did. "Some galoot can't go and steal his horse and expect to make a lot of friends."

"But Daddy *didn't* steal his horse," I argued.

"You and I know that, but most folks don't know your pa." He twirled the lasso over his head and flung it out, expertly roping a car's bumper.

I told Leo about Frank Dubois' visit to our apartment and that he'd gone from our place to see the sheriff. "I need your help," I pleaded. "We've got to find Daddy and prove he didn't steal Soapsuds."

"Well, gal, let's go investigate the scene of the crime," Leo replied. He coiled his rope and tied it to his trousers with a leather thong.

"Don't you need to tell your mama you're leaving?" I asked.

Ducking past me, he replied, "Naw, she won't worry."

As usual, he insisted on riding my bike. He'd named it "Ol' Paint" and treated it more like a horse than a bicycle. As he pedaled, he hooped and hollered as if crossing the plains on a galloping pony. With him steering and me perched on the crossbar, we set out for the ranch.

Once we reached the gate, we still had a hard ride. A long, winding, uphill road led to the house. The road cut through beautiful mountains covered with brush and piñon and pine trees. By the time we reached the polo field, where the road leveled out, Leo gasped for air. We got off and walked the rest of the way.

The ranch seemed strangely quiet, partly because the Rogers family was gone. But more than that, the roan's disappearance seemed to have robbed the place of its very heart. Mr. Rogers loved Soapsuds over any other horse in his enormous stable.

When we got to the house, we laid my bike down and looked around. It was very still. Then from far off came the growl of some kind of animal.

At once fear shone in Leo's eyes. "Didja hear that?"

"What about it?"

"It sounded like the w-wolf," he gasped. "Didn't your pa tell you about it?"

"Frank spoke something about it this morning."

"Well, that's the *last* critter I want to meet," Leo said, swallowing hard.

Leo Little Wolf handled snakes, lizards, possums, and mean stray cats, but he feared wolves over all creatures. A week ago he told me that when he lived in Arizona his oldest brother had been killed by a wolf. After that, his daddy ran off. They'd never seen him again. When I asked who lived with him in the migrant camp, he just shrugged and said, "Oh, jest Ma, some brothers and sisters, Gramma. A bunch of folks." I'd never met a one of them.

Suddenly, I heard a car coming up the road beside the polo field. I looked and spotted Frank's old, black Ford convertible rattling up the drive, coming fast and throwing dust clouds high in the air. His clattering car headed for the stable. I saw him pass, one hand on the steering wheel and the other on his battered hat. The Ford skidded to a stop and another dust cloud swirled around it.

"He's in some kinda hurry," Leo observed.

Another car, black and white, followed. The sheriff! Like Frank, the sheriff drove with one hand on the wheel. With his other hand he stuffed something into his mouth.

I nudged Leo. "Let's try to hear what the sheriff has to say."

We raced toward the stable, keeping low so Frank wouldn't see us. I wasn't sure he'd welcome me on the ranch.

The sheriff's car slowed to a stop and a man climbed out. Sheriff Slim Colley. A tall, flabby man with tight clothes, he stuffed the rest of a roll into his mouth then reached into his shirt pocket and pulled out an egg. He cracked the egg on the hood of his car.

He peeled the hard-boiled egg as he and Frank went into the stable. Leo and I sprinted across the dusty ground and halted near the door. Peeking in, I watched

Frank and the sheriff moving along the stalls, checking out the horses. Frank pointed to Soapsuds' stall. His red face grew redder. He shook his fist. I feared he was speaking harsh words about Daddy.

I tiptoed through the stable door with Leo following. Inside rose up the strong, rich smells of cut hay and horses.

Sheriff Colley said something in a low voice then popped the whole hard-boiled egg into his mouth. I heard Frank say, "He seemed trustworthy enough, but I guess he's like every other bum out here."

He *was* talking about Daddy! I wanted to shout at him, *My daddy is no bum!* I remembered back in Oklahoma how once he'd been given a dime too much change at the feed store but hadn't discovered it until he got back to the farm. Like young Abe Lincoln, he'd taken that dime and walked the four miles back to town just to plant it right into the feed store owner's palm. A man like that doesn't steal anything, least of all a horse.

If only I could tell this to the sheriff.

Frank turned and spied Leo and me crouched beside the door, straining to hear their words.

"Hey!" he shouted.

His harsh voice froze me. Leo started to take off, but I grabbed his hand. I'd never been given to running in the face of trouble, and I didn't intend to start now.

Frank rushed over to us. The sheriff followed.

"What do you think *you're* doin' here?" Frank demanded.

"Trying to find out what happened to Daddy," I said.

"Well, you've got no right to be here." His eyes shot

down. Shamed he was. Shamed for his traitorous remarks about my father.

"Sheriff, I'm George Land's daughter and I want to set the record straight," I said. "This man's filling your head with untruths about Daddy."

Frank's eyes widened. He'd always been kind to me, but at that moment he looked like he wanted to give me a good switching with a willow branch. Sweat beaded on his red face. He yanked off his bandanna and mopped his damp brow.

"My daddy couldn't have stolen that horse," I said.

The sheriff brushed egg and bread crumbs from his clothes. I noticed three blotchy stains on his shirt. "And why not, young lady?"

"Well," I began. "He's an honest Christian man. Once he walked all the way from our farm—"

"Face facts," Frank interrupted, looking me in the eye. "A horse's missing and a man's missing. It don't take much to figure that the man made off with the horse. I've tried to be patient with you, Jessie, but now you're gonna have to clear out. You're trespassing."

I turned to the other man. "Please, Sheriff, let me explain."

He eyed me beneath his bushy brows and licked his lips. Was he thinking I ought to be heard, that maybe Daddy didn't take that horse after all?

"Frank's right, young lady," he said, pulling a candy bar from his shirt pocket. "You're gonna hafta leave, sure as shootin'."

Chapter 4

"But Daddy's *innocent,*" I insisted. "Just let me explain."

The sheriff squinted down at me. Flecks of egg speckled his mouth and chin. Breathing noisily, he bit off the candy bar and, chewing, shook his head at me.

"Go on, Jessie," Frank declared. "Git home."

Leo pulled my arm. "Come on, gal."

I let Leo lead me away from the stable. We trudged back to my bike which leaned against the house. I couldn't speak because of my anger. Unfair it was! Even someone considered a mere child ought to be heard.

Leo kept quiet himself, his eyes on the ground as if looking for something he'd lost.

As we walked, I counted everything stacked against my family. Daddy and Soapsuds missing. Mama searching with many others for a job. The rent money due. Frank determined my father was a thief. And now the sheriff convinced too. If only Mr. Rogers were here. He'd give a person a fair hearing. But he wasn't due back for two whole days. If Daddy didn't turn up soon and Mama didn't find work, I might find myself back in Kansas toe-to-toe with Aunt Edna again.

I put that last thought out of my mind. With Mama busy finding a job, not one grown-up seemed set on finding Daddy and proving him innocent. That left me. I had to find him fast and show that he didn't steal Soapsuds. Otherwise he might fall into the hands of some scoundrel wanting to pin the blame on an "Okie." But where would I start?

I turned to ask Leo, but he continued to study the ground. What was it with boys? Always preoccupied with things they found in the dirt.

"What are you looking for?" I asked him.

He stopped dead still. His large black eyes glowed. "It's not what I'm lookin' for, gal. It's what I've found."

"What in the world are you talking about? Speak sensibly."

"Tracks," he explained, pointing at the ground.

I glanced down at the dirt road leading back to the stable. Tire tracks—I saw them clearly enough myself.

I shrugged. "So? There're two cars back at the stable in case you didn't notice. Now help me think. I need to figure out— "

"Stop all your thinkin' and just take a look around," he commanded. "Somethin' ain't right."

I looked at the tracks again. Maybe it took Indian eyes to see what he saw. All I saw were marks in the dirt. Marks covered by other marks.

"I don't—" I began.

"Look." He squatted on the road. I squatted beside him. "See? It looks like more than two sets of tracks."

"How can you tell?"

He sighed as if I were the dumbest person alive.

"See this set?" He pointed at one track. "That belongs to the sheriff's car."

"How do you know?" I asked.

"Because it's on top of the other tracks, and the sheriff drove up last."

OK, I understood that. "So why's this important?" I said. "I've got other things to think ab—"

"If you'd hush up a minute, gal, I'll show you somethin'," he said.

I hushed up and waited.

"I can't tell which of these other two wider tracks belongs to Frank's car. This other one's narrower, like the tracks of a trailer or somethin'."

At once I brightened. "A *horse* trailer?"

"Maybe so," Leo replied. He leaned down and traced his stubby fingers through the dirt. "This track shows a nick in the tire. And these other tracks probably belong to whatever vehicle pulled the trailer—maybe the trailer that hauled Soapsuds away."

A chill ran through me. "We've gotta show this to the sheriff!"

Leo grasped me with a firm hand. "Wait a minute. Use your noggin, gal." He pointed back at the stable. "That sheriff don't care about tire tracks. He's too busy stuffin' candy in his mouth. Let's check this out ourselves first."

Leo was right. Sheriff Colley didn't seem interested in Daddy's innocence. I'd done plenty of things on my own before. Now I was about to investigate a crime. "OK, Leo, how do we start?"

Leo smiled as he chomped his gum. "Follow the tracks with the nicked tire. Be our own posse. Might just find our horse thief by high noon."

I smiled at his hopefulness. Finding the horse thief would be fine. But where was Daddy? That's what I really wanted to know.

We left my bike behind a patch of brush and followed the tracks. They led down a dusty road beside the Rogers ranch. Leo stopped several times and studied the ground. I let him go ahead because the tracks got confusing. It looked to me like two sets of tracks.

The sun climbed into the sky. Around us rose mountains patched with scrubby brush and pine. After two weeks, I'd come to think of California as my new home. A place my family could put down roots. Maybe Mama and Daddy would have another child. Maybe—

Fool thoughts! Daddy had disappeared. If Mama didn't find a job soon, we wouldn't even have our shabby apartment anymore. Nothing'd work out right if I didn't find Daddy.

As we continued following the nicked tire tracks, I wondered who'd been driving this vehicle. Who'd have the nerve to steal Will Rogers' favorite horse?

Abruptly, the tracks stopped.

"What happened?" I asked Leo.

"The vehicle stopped here," he said. "Looks like it turned 'round and went back the way it come. That explains the two sets of tracks on the road."

I saw a jumble of tire tracks, which I guessed marked the spot the car turned around. I also saw something else.

Hoofprints! And footprints!

"Look at *this!*" I exclaimed.

"Yep, I see it," Leo replied, scratching his wild hair.

"Did the thief take Soapsuds out of the trailer here?" I wondered aloud.

"Looks like it," Leo said.

"But where'd they go?"

On the left, a thicket grew up and blocked us. On the right, the road ended and the land plunged almost straight down. I looked over the edge into a deep, rugged ravine. Then I spotted something.

"What's that down there?" I asked.

Leo joined me at the edge. "What's what?"

"That blue thing." I pointed at something caught in the brush below.

I sat and began to edge myself down, but Leo caught my arm.

"Hey, gal, *watch* it," he warned. "You can't go down there. You'll break your neck."

"It might be a clue. I'm going down."

"Too steep," my friend cautioned. "Besides, you know what critters hang around ravines? *Wolves.*"

When I set my mind to something, I was not easily swayed. Even the threat of wolves would not keep me from a clue that might lead to Daddy.

"I'm going," I said firmly.

Leo shrugged and took the rope from his belt. He tied one end around my waist and held tight to the other end as I lowered myself down the side.

I skidded down the slope. Small clouds of dust billowed up. I clung to the dirt and the rock under me and tasted the grit in my teeth. I dodged some prickly looking plants growing on the side of the ravine.

Leo called down, "I'm runnin' out of rope up here."

"Almost there," I sang out.

I dropped the last couple of feet to a level but narrow ledge. Below, the ravine dropped away steep. There wasn't enough rope in all of Will Rogers' ranch to lower me down there. The blue thing hung snagged in a patch of brush just beyond the ledge. I swallowed hard and wiped my sweaty hands on my overalls. I remembered how, not long ago in Arizona, I had had to climb out of a flooded arroyo a lot less steep than this.

Stepping carefully, I made my way along the ledge.

"Watch it, gal," cried Leo, "those ledges crumble easy!"

I put his warning out of my mind. I could see now that the blue thing was a piece of cloth.

Up ahead the ledge came to an end. I reached out to try to grab the cloth, but it hung just beyond my grasp. Clinging to the ravine wall, I inched my body out as far as I could without pitching over the edge. Face to the wall, I smelled the rock and dust and dry brush warming in the sun. My mouth pressed against the dirt. It tasted bitter.

Glancing into the ravine, I caught sight of something

else—a gray blur, gliding through the brush. Then it disappeared. *The wolf?*

I turned my attention back to the cloth. Stretching my fingertips, I could just touch the brush. I grabbed for a branch and pulled. With it came the blue cloth. My fingers slid down the prickly branch toward the cloth. Just a few more inches and I'd have it. My foot slipped and I gasped, but I managed to get balanced again.

"*Jessie!*" yelled Leo from above. I felt the rope pull tight around me. If I pitched over the edge, I might well yank Leo into the ravine with me.

I held my breath and tried again. Leaning even farther, I reached out. This time when I grasped the branch, my fingertips touched the cloth!

Stretching, stretching, I managed to get my fingers around the cloth. As I pulled it back, I wadded it into my hand. Then I inched backward until, finally, I got back to the spot on the ledge where I had first landed. Grinning up at Leo, I waved the blue cloth. I saw him wipe his forehead on his sleeve as he chewed his gum furiously.

Then I examined the scrap.

It was a piece of shirt sleeve, with a cuff, but no button. I ran my scratched fingertips over the rough blue cotton. The exact same color as one of Daddy's shirts.

I remembered something. The shirt Daddy had been wearing yesterday. His blue cotton shirt missing a button on the cuff. Mama wanted to sew on a button, but Daddy said he'd just roll up his sleeves.

This scrap *had* to be from Daddy's shirt!

Turning the fabric over, I spied some reddish-brown stains along the edge of the cuff.

Bloodstains!

Chapter 5

For the longest time I stood on that ledge staring down at the bloodied scrap of blue cloth. Not just any scrap, though. A piece of my father's shirt. *Daddy's been hurt, hurt bad,* I kept thinking. My whole body went numb, as if I didn't know where I was, or even who I was.

Leo's shouting reached me. I glanced up. He tugged the rope and called for me to climb. I folded the cloth carefully and stuffed it under the bib of my overalls.

Finally, I stretched up, clutching the rope. As Leo pulled, I dug the toes of my shoes into the dirt, one step at a time. My legs felt limp and useless but, inch by inch, Leo dragged me up that ravine.

When I got to the top, dust powdered my clothes, my face, my hands. I didn't care. I just sat there, my feet dangling over the edge, staring beyond the ravine and the brush and trees to the other side. I caught a glimpse of some Santa Monica rooftops. I thought, *Mama's down there somewhere, thinking things will be better once she's got a job. Thinking Daddy will be coming home soon.* I felt an aching, a powerful longing for Daddy to be with me and an awful fear that he might never be.

Leo's gasping brought me back from my thoughts. I turned around and saw him lying on the ground.

"Gal," he huffed, "don't—never—do—that—again!"

I scrambled to my feet and rushed over to him. The poor kid had plumb wore himself out. His dark face dripped with sweat. His hands still clenched the rope.

I pried his fingers loose and helped him up. After a moment he got his breath back.

"OK, since you had to go down there, what did you find?" he demanded. "And it better be good."

I didn't think I could stand to look at that piece of cloth again. But I brought it out and handed it to him. I turned away and tried to think about something else.

I thought about how Daddy once made me a wagon when we lived in Oklahoma. I thought about his smell—a kind of sawdust and soap smell. I thought about his smile. . . .

"What is this?" Leo asked.

Facing him, I said, "A piece of Daddy's shirt. It's got bloodstains on it."

Leo's eyes searched my face. He handled the cloth with his fingertips, as if he couldn't bear to touch it anymore.

Handing it back to me, he said, "There's lots of blue shirts, gal. This could belong to anyone."

"It's *Daddy's,*" I insisted. I didn't want to say the rest, how I was sure Daddy lay hurt somewhere. If I didn't say it out loud, it didn't seem quite real.

At that moment, a dusty, green car with yellow, spoked wheels chugged up the road and skidded to a stop a few feet from where we stood. For a minute the driver sat behind the wheel just watching us. I felt uneasy.

"Who is it?" I asked Leo. He shrugged.

Finally, the driver opened the door and climbed out. He was a thin man with brown hair and dark spectacles, dressed in a wrinkled, brown suit and a matching felt hat. With his hands on his hips, he seemed to be sizing us up.

He smiled at us, though more grimace than smile, like he was in pain. "What're you squirts up to?" he spoke in a sharp, biting voice that betrayed his smile.

Neither of us spoke. He stepped toward us.

Suddenly I remembered the scrap of cloth and hid it behind my back.

"You squirts know there's been a crime on this ranch?" the man asked.

"We know a man's disappeared," I said. I didn't much care for this stranger calling us squirts.

"And a horse," the man added. He came closer. I watched as his jaw tensed. "So what're you doing here?"

Something about the man angered me. I said, "If it's any business of yours, mister, we're looking for clues."

His jaw tensed again.

I went on, "We're trying to find out where that horse went and what became of Daddy—"

I gasped at my slip. *Jessie Land, you little fool!*

The man grinned. He pointed at me with a long, thin finger. "So your father's the horse thief, eh?"

I felt my face heat up. "My father is no criminal. You clearly don't know a thing about it."

The grin disappeared as the man reached into his pocket. He produced a wallet, opened it, and flashed some kind of card at us. I couldn't make it out.

"Deputy Smith, sheriff's office," he announced. His voice and the way he stood told me that he thought himself pretty important. "I know more than you think, Miss Land."

"I've never seen the likes of you before," Leo said.

"And I've never seen the likes of you before neither," Deputy Smith told him. "Listen, we're conducting an investigation here. We don't need squirts getting in the way. Both of you get on home."

Since he'd already called Daddy a horse thief, I knew I needed to set him straight.

"We've already found some important clues," I said.

"Oh? Like what?"

I wished I could look into his eyes so I could be sure of his intentions. I forced myself to tell him our story in case he might be able to help find Daddy and clear him of wrongdoing.

With the scrap of cloth still hid behind my back, I pointed at the tire tracks.

"We followed the tracks of this horse trailer," I said. "One tire has a nick in it. Leo tracked the trailer from the stable at the ranch."

Deputy Smith knelt down and studied the track. His jaw tensed. When he stood up, he grinned again. "Good work!"

He meant that, surely. Encouraged, I pulled out the

scrap of blue cloth.

"I found this down in that ravine. It's just like the shirt Daddy was wearing when he disappeared. And look—" I turned it over. "Bloodstains."

Deputy Smith took the cloth and examined it carefully. He held it up to the light, as if trying to look through it.

"Those bloodstains mean Daddy's hurt," I explained. "He couldn't have stolen Soapsuds. He was probably trying to *stop* the horse thief."

Cocking his head, the deputy replied, "You're right. This's important evidence."

I brightened. "So what'll we do now?"

Smiling, he said, "I'll radio the sheriff and get him over here to see this for himself. We'll see if we can trace these trailer tires. And we'll have some lab folks take a look at this cloth." He grinned at me, but I wished I'd kept ahold of the scrap. "You two go on home. We'll find the thief—and we'll find your father too, young lady."

We let him lead us back down the road past his car.

"Thanks for your help," he said.

We walked away. After a while, Leo stopped and looked at me, frowning. He turned and gazed back. The deputy leaned against his car, watching us.

"I didn't see no police radio in that lawman's car."

"It's probably hidden," I suggested, "so his car doesn't look like a police car."

"It don't look nothin' like no police car," he said. "I think we oughta get back to the ranch and tell the sheriff and Frank about him."

I nodded and we ran back along the rutted dirt road.

When we reached the ranch, the sun was well up in the sky and the day had grown hot. Sweat poured from my forehead and my legs ached.

I noticed the sheriff's car was gone. I saw Frank leading one of Mr. Rogers' horses into the corral. His red face turned the color of a plum at our approach. He was none too happy to see me again.

After putting the horse in the corral, he dropped the lead in the dirt, and stomped over to us.

"Jessie Land, I thought the sheriff and I both told you to leave," he declared, his eyes narrowing.

I forced myself to speak respectful. "I know what you told me. But Leo and I found clues that prove Daddy—"

"Git off this property," he commanded. "I know you're concerned for your father, but don't make me call the sheriff."

"That's just what I *want* you to do," I told him.

His expression went from anger to bewilderment. *"Huh?"*

"I want the sheriff to see what we found," I declared.

He took off his bandanna and mopped his brow.

"The sheriff didn't even take a look around," I said. "Leo and I found some tracks."

Suspicion clouded Frank's face. "Tracks? What kind of tracks?"

Leo stepped in and explained about the trailer tracks and how they led down a dirt road beside the Rogers ranch.

"That road don't go nowhere," Frank grumbled.

"Well, that's where the tracks lead," Leo insisted. "And Jessie here found something else."

Suddenly I wished I hadn't given away the bloodied scrap of blue cloth. But I told Frank about it, then about the sheriff's deputy turning up.

Frank's face eased back to its normal red. "Deputy?"

"Deputy Smith," I told him. "Said he was investigating the disappearances."

"Never heard of a Deputy Smith," Frank admitted.

I went on, "That piece of shirt with blood on it proves something bad happened. We've got to find Daddy *now.*"

Frank scratched his head. Then he eyed me carefully. "All right, we'll have a look." Then he warned, "But if you're making this up, you'll be plenty sorry."

Frank fetched his trampled hat from a fencepost and herded Leo and me into his car. We set out for the dirt road.

Frank said nothing as he steered his car on the rutted path. Neither did Leo or I. But when we neared the place where we'd talked to Deputy Smith, my heart started pounding. Swallowing hard, I turned in panic to Leo.

The deputy's car was gone!

"Stop here," I said.

Frank tromped on his brake and the Ford skidded to a stop. A dust cloud rose above us and wavered off into the sky.

Leo and I climbed out and looked around.

When I gazed down at the ground, fear raged through

me like a fire sweeping a forest.

"Where's that deputy fella?" Frank asked, getting out of the car.

Not only had Deputy Smith disappeared, but something else was terribly, terribly wrong.

"Look at the road, Leo," I cried. "Look!"

"Oh, no!" I heard him groan.

The tire tracks were gone.

Chapter 6

I stood stunned on that dirt road. I kept thinking, *Jessie Land, that "deputy" was a plain fraud and you trusted him. Foolish girl! Now how will you help your daddy?*

Frank's words broke through to me.

"OK, Jessie, enough of your tricks. Get in the car and I'll fetch you back to your bike. Then, you stay clear of this ranch. Understand?"

"But there *was* a man here, Frank," I insisted.

"She's tellin' the truth," Leo chimed in.

Pointing at the road, I added, "He must've smoothed out the tracks. And I did find a scrap of—"

"Enough!" Frank barked, tearing off his rumpled hat. His gray eyes flamed at me. "Because of your father, I'll likely lose my job, unless I find that horse."

Instead of angering me, his words made me pity him. Suddenly I understood. He feared getting fired because of Soapsuds. His own future was tied to finding the horse.

Back in the car, as Frank drove, Leo spouted out, "That fella must of dragged somethin' behind his car to wipe out those tracks. So we gotta be on to somethin'. He wouldn't erase tire tracks 'less they mattered."

When we got back, Frank climbed out of his car and stalked away. He'd already had his say.

Leo and I headed for my bike.

"Those tracks must of been a real important clue," my friend said.

"Yes, and I know just what I need to do now."

"What?" Leo asked, his dark eyes on me.

"Talk to the sheriff."

"I'll go with you," he said, untying the rope from his trousers and spinning a lasso over his head.

What a blessing this boy was! It was like we'd been friends forever, even though I'd known him a scant two weeks.

Leo steered and pedaled my bike. I perched on the crossbar. At least going to town was mainly downhill.

On the way into Santa Monica I kept trying to solve the puzzle of who really took Soapsuds. Someone needing money might've taken him, hoping Mr. Rogers would pay a lot to get him back. Or maybe someone just wanted something the famous Will Rogers owned. And what about "Deputy Smith"? He was somehow involved in the theft since he took the scrap of shirt and also wiped out those tracks on the road. But Daddy—how did he fit into this? And where was he now?

It was well past noon when we rode into Santa Monica. Up ahead I spied a cannery, an old, corrugated iron building, with a sign out front: *Hiring for 2 jobs today only.* A dusty line of silent, sad-looking people wound out the front door, down the street, threaded through an alley, and around the block. I looked for Mama in the line but didn't see her. Gazing at those folks, I felt shame at not looking for a job myself, at letting Mama go off by herself to find work. So far, all I'd done was get into trouble.

But I had a job—finding Daddy and proving him innocent. And I had to find him before the sheriff found him and locked him away like a common thief.

As we neared the sheriff's office, a green car with yellow, spoked wheels rumbled past us.

The "deputy"!

"Leo, stop!" I cried, pointing at the dusty, green car.

Leo braked and just about threw me over the handlebars.

"What?" he said.

"That Deputy Smith fellow. There he goes."

It took only a second for me to decide what to do. "Come on, follow him. *Hurry!*"

Leo sparked to life. Letting out a whoop, he pushed off and pedaled hard. He gasped for breath as we trailed the car.

I saw the car turn left about four blocks ahead.

"Hurry, Leo!" I yelled. "We'll lose him!"

The bicycle shook as Leo pumped harder. The rubber wheel and wooden wheel bounced and slammed over bumps in the street. I grew excited, but when we reached the place where Smith had turned, my heart broke. No sign of the car. Before us stood a row of old buildings, most of them boarded up or plastered with FORECLOSED signs.

Leo coasted to a stop, panting. I hopped off the bike and stood at the corner trying to figure out where the villain had gone.

Then I heard the ticking. The kind of ticking hot metal makes. I remembered the sound from when I lived in Liberal, Kansas, with my aunt and her family. They ran a gas station and cars stopping for gas there had made the same sound.

I followed the sound. Only a few feet away, I found Smith's car parked in a narrow alley beside one of the buildings, one of the few old buildings without a FORECLOSED sign.

"Hey, gal, wait up," Leo gasped.

I spun around and hushed him.

I crept along the building to a window, the glass thickly covered with dust. Pulling a bandanna from my overalls pocket, I wiped off a corner of the window. Then I peeked in. I made out stacks of boxes in the dim light.

I wanted to get inside and find "Deputy Smith." If only I could get that shirt scrap back, then I might be able to convince the sheriff of Daddy's innocence.

I stole alongside the building to a paint-blistered gray door. Putting my ear to it, I listened. I heard a voice on the other side. I couldn't go in that way.

As I started to ease away, a hand grabbed my shoulder.

I choked back a scream as Leo's voice came at me, "He in there?"

My heart raced. I turned and grabbed Leo's shirt and declared, "Don't *ever* do that again, boy!"

He followed me down the alley. Near a pile of smashed boxes I discovered a ground-level window. A piece of the glass about the size of baseball had been broken out, but the window was locked. I could see the latch. I thought a minute, then decided.

I turned and said, "Wait here. I'm going inside."

"Oh no you ain't," Leo replied. "Not alone leastwise. I'll go too."

"Leo, it'll be a lot more dangerous out here. Smith is sure to come flying out any second. You need to lay in wait for him, just in case. Better get your rope ready."

Leo grinned. He touched the rope tied to his trousers. "You want me to rope and hog-tie the varmint?"

I shook my head. "Just watch for him. Or others. There'll likely be others."

Leo's eyes widened. He unhitched his rope.

Lord, please forgive me for stretching the truth, I prayed silently. I squatted beside the window. After wrapping my hand with my bandanna to protect it from the jagged glass, I reached through the hole and felt for the latch. I knew one sudden move could slash my wrist.

"*Gal!*" Leo whispered loudly.

I jerked and nearly cut my wrist. I ignored Leo and kept after the latch. It moved!

"Hurry, gal, someone's coming!" Leo dashed to the other side of the alley and hid behind a mound of trash.

Shutting my eyes, I yanked hard. I felt the glass bite my wrist. *Ow!* Then I heard footsteps near the alley's entrance.

With all my strength I tugged at the latch. It gave way in my hand. My wrist slid along the glass, leaving a smear of blood. I pulled my hand out through the hole, not even stopping to inspect my injury, hoisted up the window, and scrambled inside the building.

I bumped against a stack of wooden crates. Above me, a large window in the roof cast a dim light in the place.

The wound on my wrist stung like the dickens, so I wrapped the bandanna more tightly around it.

I stood still and listened. Nothing. The footsteps outside must have just been someone walking along the sidewalk out front.

I stepped around stacks of crates. Some were stamped THIS SIDE UP. On others I read FURNITURE or LAMPS or PILLOWS. The room smelled of dusty wood and mildew.

When I came to a door, I paused. I heard no one, but what if Smith stood just on the other side? What if he lay in wait for me?

Well, what if he did? I refused to let fear stop me now. I just *had* to get that scrap of Daddy's shirt back. I swallowed hard and held my breath. Gripping the knob, I turned it. The door silently eased open.

I slipped through into an enormous room. To my right I saw the three dirty windows on the alley side of the building. The only real light came from a naked bulb hanging from the ceiling on the other side of the room. Beneath that light, his back to me, Smith leaned against a small desk and talked on the telephone. Pure fright rushed through me as I stared at his back.

Stacked boxes formed a kind of maze between me and him. I sneaked from stack to stack, stepping lightly on the wooden floor. I saw Smith start to turn and I ducked behind a box. Even inside he wore those dark glasses of his. What sense did that make? I could hear his villainous voice.

"Trouble?" he said. "Naw. Not much trouble. I got it from her."

I heard him tap the desk beside him. Peeking around the corner of the box, I saw what I'd come for on the desk. The blue shirt scrap!

"Just a minute," he said into the mouthpiece. He set the phone down and switched on an electric fan. The blades rattled and began spinning. He smiled, holding his head back like he'd never known anything so fine as standing in front of that fan.

Phone back in hand, he said, "Tomorrow night, OK. A little fire, right. Just enough to scare 'em. They'll clear out faster'n you can say 'Okie dokie.' " His vile laugh hung in the air as he clunked down the telephone.

Whatever did he mean? What "little fire"? Who did he plan to scare?

I pushed his confusing words from my mind. My eyes fastened onto the cloth on the desk. I had to get it!

I crouched down, my damp hands clutching the side of the crate. My mouth went dry. I watched the cloth and Smith and waited.

Smith went to the door. I panicked. What if Leo stood

right on the other side? But the villain didn't open the door. He just stood there facing it, as if thinking about something.

My chance!

Heading for the desk, I took careful but quick steps. Then I made a big mistake. I took my eyes off what lay ahead and looked at Smith.

I never saw the cord. But I felt my foot snag something. I tripped but caught myself before pitching headlong onto the floor. *Jessie Land, you fool!* The electric fan tottered and fell. It made an awful racket in that warehouse building, screeching as it struck the floor and then whining horribly.

Smith spun around. He flashed his dreadful grin right at me, like a weapon.

Chapter 7

I couldn't move. Smith's vile grin froze me to the spot. The fallen fan made a horrible grinding noise on the floor, but Smith made no move to fetch it.

Something inside me said, *You're not caught yet. Grab that shirt scrap and run to the sheriff's office—now!*

I took a step toward the desk, but Smith lunged forward. In a flash he snatched up the scrap and stuffed it in his jacket pocket.

He flashed that evil grin at me again.

"Well, well," he said over the clatter of the fan.

I didn't wait to hear his next words. I turned to run. In front of me loomed the dark maze of boxes. Which way had I come? How could I escape? The villain behind me didn't give me time to stop and think. I shot forward, weaving 'round the stacks of boxes, trying to find the door.

My head pounded and icy panic swept through me as I dodged this way and that. I heard Smith close behind. He gasped, "I'll get you, squirt. Just you wait!"

Suddenly I spotted it. The door! I bolted through into the dim room. A patch of light on the floor led me to the window.

From the larger room Smith called out, "You can't hide from me!"

I had only seconds. I jerked up the window with my bandanna-wrapped hand. In my hurry, I didn't get a good grip. *BANG!* The window crashed closed. Glass shattered around me with an awful racket.

Oh no! He'll find me now!

I dropped to the floor, yanked up the window frame, and scooted through the opening.

Out in the alley I glanced around. No Leo. Where'd that boy go? I dashed for my bicycle. A hissing noise came from Smith's car.

"Hey, gal, wait up!"

Leo!

I spun around and spotted my wild-haired friend squatting beside the car. The hissing noise came from the tire as Leo let the air out.

"Quick!" I cried. "He's coming!"

Leo hopped to his feet. I was already on my bike, so he sprang to the crossbar. I pushed off with every ounce of strength I had.

Then, unexpectedly, Smith shot out of nowhere and dived for us. "I'll get you little squirts!" I felt his hand grabbing my arm. We couldn't get caught by this rascal!

"Vamoose, you outlaw!" Leo shouted at the varmint.

Leo's cry must have startled him because Smith jumped back. I took off, swerving around him. Then he lurched for us again. This time his shoes skidded on the pavement. He stumbled and fell and I nearly ran over his arm.

I pumped the pedals like crazy, but it seemed as if we barely moved. Glancing back, I saw Smith angrily kicking his car's tires.

Leo craned his neck around, watching for signs of the villain. "Let's find us a hideout," he said. "That varmint's name ain't Smith. I looked at his car registration. It's Joe Beck. That ain't no police car and Beck ain't no deputy neither."

"Joe Beck? Well, it's an outlaw's name if I ever heard one," I declared.

Foolish child! Why did you trust him with that scrap of Daddy's shirt?

Just then I spotted Hoppers store up ahead.

Yes! Mr. Hopper'd always been nice to me. That would be a safe place to hide. We jumped off the bike as I coasted into the alley beside the store.

"See anyone?" I asked Leo.

He peered out the alley. "Nope."

I hid my bike behind a stack of barrels. Then Leo and I hurried to the front door of the store. Still no sign of Joe Beck. But I knew he was around. Somewhere.

We ducked inside. The bell tinkled lightly. I heard Mr. Hopper's voice in the back of the store. The red bicycle stood in the window. It was as lovely as ever, but I concerned myself now with hiding from Beck.

Tugging at Leo's shirt, I urged, "Come on. Let's get away from the window or he'll see us for sure."

As we moved to the back, Mr. Hopper's voice grew louder and clearer.

"I understand," he said, "but I'm telling you you'll have it on Monday. It's not my fault. These ranches canceled a big order. What else can I do? It'll just take longer to get the payment together."

There were more words, then I heard the telephone being hung up. When Mr. Hopper came out from the back of the store, he looked worried. That look changed to alarm when he spied Leo and me hiding behind some bolts of cloth.

At that same instant, I glanced out the window and saw Beck walking toward the store. We were about to be caught!

Stepping back and pulling Leo with me, I said, "We're just looking, Mr. Hopper."

Mr. Hopper smiled slightly. He fussed with his blond moustache and then dug a hand into his pocket and jingled his change.

"Go right ahead." Then he looked hard at me. "Say, your face is mighty red. Have you been running?"

"Just riding my bicycle, sir," I told him.

Tugging Leo with me, I eased away from Mr. Hopper. I found a spot where I could see out the window but couldn't be seen by anyone looking in. We hunched beside a rack of men's shirts. I touched a dark blue one, like the one Daddy had been wearing. Like the scrap of cloth I'd found. The scrap of cloth Beck still had.

Beck appeared on the other side of the store's window. He gazed in!

I ducked out of the way. Turning, I spied Mr. Hopper

watching the man. He wore a look of disapproval on his face. I sensed he didn't care for that man either. If he only knew what I did!

Peeking at the window again, I saw Beck walk away.

Some other people came into the store and Mr. Hopper went to wait on them.

Leo and I remained in the back for a long time.

Finally, my friend whispered, "Can't we git out now?"

"We can try," I replied.

We slipped past Mr. Hopper and his customers. He shot us a brief glance. I saw worry still etched on his face.

Outside I glanced around. No sign of Beck. Quickly, we climbed back on my bike.

"Let's get to the sheriff's and tell him about that Beck fellow," I said.

We pedaled the few blocks to the sheriff's office. Then we hopped off the bike and ran smack into the sheriff as he stepped out of the door licking a double scoop chocolate ice-cream cone.

"Whoa, you two," he bellowed, "watch where you're goin'. You nearly made me drop my sweets."

It looked like he'd already dropped it once. A large chocolate stain smudged his shirt pocket. I'd never seen a man so prone to soil himself. I pitied Sheriff Slim Colley's wife. She had herself a full-time job with the laundry.

"Sheriff, I've got to talk to you," I said.

His mouth turned down. He replied, "No time, child. I'm off to form a posse."

A posse! I pictured Daddy being hunted down like a real

moving picture desperado. I asked fearfully, "Does this have to do with Mr. Rogers' missing horse?"

I don't think he recognized me until that moment. "Oh, you're that . . . ah, Land's daughter, ain't you? Well, never you mind, child. I'll find your pa sure as shootin'."

"Daddy didn't take that horse," I blurted out. "Frank Dubois lied about that."

He tried moving around us, but I stepped sideways and stood my ground.

"Listen here, child, this's none of your affair," he grumbled. "I've got official business to conduct."

"It's my business too," I insisted. "It has to do with my father."

"You *gotta* listen to her, Sheriff," Leo spouted. "She found proof that her pa's no horse thief."

This news didn't seem to surprise him. "She did, huh?" he said, taking a big bite of the ice-cream cone. "And just what might this proof be?"

"Well, a man pretending to be a deputy took it from me," I answered. "But we know where he—"

"I've gotta go," he said. "I'm late already."

I worried that this man, who could help me, wouldn't even hear me out. I pleaded, "Two minutes. Just give me two minutes of your time. Please, Sheriff."

I've noticed that some adults cannot abide a begging youngster. I hoped the sheriff was one of them. As he worked on the ice-cream cone, he seemed to mull over my offer. Finally, he nodded toward his office. "Come inside. You've got your two minutes. Not a mite longer."

We stepped inside. The sheriff's office took up a narrow space between a furniture store and a dentist's office. I wondered where he locked criminals up, where he would have locked up Daddy if he'd caught him.

"The clock's a-tickin'," the sheriff said.

Quick as I could, I explained to him about me and Leo finding the nicked tire tracks, finding the scrap of Daddy's shirt, then Beck showing up. I told him about seeing Beck in town and following him to the warehouse. Then about getting chased. When I finished, I may've taken more than two minutes, but the sheriff knew the whole story. Now, for certain, he'd go after that Joe Beck.

The sheriff squinted at me. Then he did something strange. He smiled. I hoped it meant he believed me. And he planned to help.

"Child, I'd chase after you too if you broke into my place," he declared.

I felt the blood drain from my face. *No!*

"Listen here. I don't need any juvenile helping me investigate this crime. I understand your wanting to help your pa and all. But it's time to accept what's obvious. Your pa's guilty. Guilty as sin."

"But what about Joe Beck?" Leo burst in. "He pretended to be a lawman, didn't he?"

"So you say," the sheriff replied, "and that would be a violation of the law. But I don't have time to look into that right now. Fact is, George Land's the horse thief, sure as shootin'."

"No!" I cried. "Daddy'd never steal anything."

The sheriff eyed me carefully, gave his melting ice-cream cone a few licks, then went behind his desk. He opened a drawer and pulled out a large envelope. With sticky chocolate fingers he took out a yellow sheet of paper out of the envelope. Flattening the paper on his desk, he motioned me over to see it.

"All right, child," he said as I joined him behind the desk. "You tell me. Who wrote this note?"

I looked down and read the message scrawled in pencil.

> Will Rogers:
>
> I got your horse Soapsuds and I'm taking good care of him. If you want him back safe and sound, get $10,000 together right away. I'll let you know where to leave it and where to find your horse.

I couldn't take my eyes off that note. Tears trailed down my cheeks, dripping onto the desk. *No! No! No!* I shook my head, but in my heart I knew the truth.

It was Daddy's handwriting!

Chapter 8

"It's your pa's handwriting, ain't it?" the sheriff asked. "Frank said it was."

Unable to admit the truth, I shook my head. *It couldn't be,* I told myself. *Daddy wouldn't–*

"Ain't it?" the sheriff repeated.

In my hurt, I wanted to lash out at the man. I snapped, "You'd do well, Sheriff, to go back to school. Then you wouldn't be using words like 'ain't.' " But inside I wanted to cry. I longed to wake up and find this nothing more than an awful, awful dream!

Stung by my words, Sheriff Colley stepped back. His ice-cream cone had melted all over his hand. He tried finishing it off, then became disgusted. He threw the whole mess into a trash can and wiped his hands on his pant leg. "Go on and get outta here, you. I've got a horse thief to hunt down."

He tucked the ransom note back into the envelope and dropped it in his desk drawer. Then sizing me up, he closed the drawer and locked it. Now he had me pegged as a thief!

Leo had stood behind me all this time. I turned,

grabbed him, and dragged him out the door with me. I felt shaky, like any minute I'd start bawling like a big baby.

Outside I let loose of my friend and mumbled, "I've gotta get home, Leo. You'd best go home yourself."

"But, gal–"

"Just go on," I argued. "Your mama's probably worried sick, wondering where you are."

Without even giving him a glance, I jumped on my bike and raced up the street, my tears flying behind me. My head hurt with the thoughts that occupied it. Thoughts on top of thoughts, like the tire tracks I'd seen at the ranch that morning. One second I believed Daddy would never steal a horse, that he'd never write a horrible ransom note like that. Then, the next second, I nearly believed the worst of my father. After all, his hand had written those words. Maybe–

No! How could I question his honesty? He didn't steal that horse. There had to be another explanation.

The tears on my face dried as I rode around three long lines of folks hoping to get jobs. On the side of a building someone had painted yet another nasty warning: OKIES CLEAR OUT NOW OR ELSE! But I couldn't think about that. I didn't want to think about anything just then. I wanted to get home. Home to our safe little apartment. Home to Mama. She would be there waiting and I could tell her everything. She'd know exactly what to do.

I wheeled my bike to the back of the apartment building and coasted to a stop beside our old, broken-down Essex. Propping my bicycle against our car, I dashed through the rusty screen door, letting it slam shut behind me.

Inside, the smells of dirty laundry and cooked cabbage filled the hall. What a horrid odor! I held my breath and hustled to our door. No sound came from inside and when I tried the door it was still locked.

Slumping against the door, I breathed in the vile smells in the hall. *Mama, where are you?* I took the key hanging from a string around my neck and unlocked the door.

The apartment felt so quiet and empty I almost started crying again. It seemed like weeks since Frank had been in this very room telling Mama and me that Daddy was a horse thief. None of it seemed real.

For a moment I stared at one wall where someone had thumbtacked a bunch of bent postcards. Since they covered a hole, Mama never saw fit to take them down. One showed a foamy, blue sea lapping a beach with the words, *See the Pacific Ocean in 1933!* Another had a picture of an orange grove. The words read, *California—a Garden Paradise.*

I cut myself a thick slice of bread and plopped down at our dining room table. It wobbled when I leaned my arms against it. I tried hard to think, to figure out a way to find Daddy and Soapsuds.

Everyone believed Daddy to be a horse thief—Frank, the sheriff, probably everybody in the whole town. My father the horse thief.

I took a bite of bread, but it clumped in my throat as if it might choke me.

Not knowing what to do next, I lay down on the thread-bare, gray couch to wait for Mama. At once, I felt very tired. I closed my eyes just for a minute. Just long enough. . . .

* * *

Tap tap tap.

"Hey, girl, you in there?"

From my black dream a sound at the door roused me. *Where am I?*

Tap tap tap.

"Girl! I ain't got all day."

The apartment, Mama, Daddy's disappearance, Will Rogers' horse missing—the events of the day swirled through my mind and jerked me fully awake. How long had I slept?

I got up and went to the door. Opening it, I found Mrs. Jackman, the landlady, standing with a ladle in one hand. She scowled at me. Her wide mouth twisted into a grimace and her long, thin nose aimed at me like a pointing finger. Some greenish-brown stuff dripped from the ladle onto the floor of the hall.

"Where you been, girl?" she demanded. "I been knocking a full five minutes. Your ma told me you'd—"

At word of Mama's name I felt something like an electric shock. *"Mama?"* I asked her. "Where is she?"

Mrs. Jackman's scowl grew fierce. "How should I know? She called on the telephone in my apartment. She gave me a message for you."

The landlady stepped past me into our apartment, dripping ladle and all. She said, "I won't abide this use of my telephone. I'm no public telephone company, I'll have you know."

"What did Mama say?" I asked eagerly.

Mrs. Jackman squinted at the apartment and at me like she found nothing she could approve of. But I remembered that she had six children in an apartment no larger than ours. Maybe all those people together had soured her.

"She said she'd be late," the landlady told me, still squinting. "She said there were long lines everywhere. She might not be home till dark."

"What else did she say?" I said. How I wished I'd been in Mrs. Jackman's apartment to talk with Mama myself. I longed to tell her all that Leo and I had discovered.

Mrs. Jackman stuck her unpleasant face close to mine and said sharply, "That's it. She had to hang up quick 'cause she was calling from some store. But listen here, I gotta talk to that ma of yours. When she gets home."

I nodded.

"Don't you forget," she commanded. "It's important, seeing's what your pa's gone and done."

I jumped, startled at her words. *"Daddy?* What do you know about my daddy?"

The landlady crossed her arms. The stuff from the ladle dripped onto her faded print dress. The hostile woman glared at me.

"Your pa's a horse thief, that much I know. He's gone and stole something from the nicest man in town, the nicest man anywhere." She almost smiled.

The Jackmans knew Will Rogers. According to her, a few years back, he'd given her husband a loan. When Mr. Jackman couldn't pay the money back, Mr. Rogers said, "I don't rightly recollect givin' you nothin', so your business is to pay me back nothin'." It sounded just like Mr. Rogers.

The scowl returned to her face.

"I don't take to having criminals under my roof," she said. Her mouth puckered up like she'd just gulped down a spoonful of vinegar.

"Daddy's no criminal," I said. "I have proof—or I did have proof." I saw no need to go into the details with her.

"Mr. Rogers' horse is missing and so's your pa," she spat. "That sure suggests criminal behavior to me."

I looked hard at her. It angered me that all these people jumped to conclusions about my father. It just wasn't right!

"Daddy's missing because he got hurt somehow," I told her. "I know who's involved in this and I aim to—"

"I don't care to hear the opinions of a child, do you hear? I was gonna tell your ma, but I'll just tell you. I want the lot of you out of this apartment."

A chill ran through me. "But—"

"I won't listen to arguments," the landlady said. "You and your ma be out by Sunday or I'll call the police and have you thrown out. We got us a respectable apartment house here, and I plan to keep it that way."

"But—but—" What could I say?

The woman went to the door and stood in the hall. "You'd best be packing, girl."

Tears sprang to my eyes. "You don't understand."

"I understand the law," she said. "What's right and what's wrong. Don't you forget. *Sunday!*"

Chapter 9

I shut the door and slumped against it. I gazed at the furniture in our apartment. All worn and threadbare, some of it broken, none of it ours. This was no home, not a real one leastwise.

Draped over a rickety chair two of Daddy's faded shirts waited for Mama or me to iron. I crossed the room, sat in the chair, and ran my fingers over the rough fabric. I thought of the scrap of Daddy's shirt I'd found. Three shirts. That's all he had. I examined the cuffs. Yes, and all of them frayed. *We're poor,* I thought, my heart aching. *We have nothing. These troubles rise up because of poverty.*

At that moment Leo burst into the apartment, shaking me from my gloom.

"Gal, lookit what I found!" he cried, waving a sheet of yellow paper. "I found bunches of 'em all over the camp."

I took the sheet and read:

MIGRANTS CLEAR OUT!

Santa Monica already has problems enough with this Depression without you adding to them. There arent enough jobs. There arent enough places to live and your Hooverville camps aren't welcome. Go back to where you came from. The citizens of Santa Monica don't want higher taxes to keep you here. Go home now or face the consequences!

"What 'consequences'?" I asked.

He huffed. "Heard a rumor some folks from town might try somethin' tomorrow night."

"Try what?"

"Burn out the camp," he said. He didn't look at me. He just stared at his scuffed shoes.

Jessie Land, I told myself, *you're not the only person in the world with a problem. What's poor Leo and his family going to do?*

I put my arm around him. Then an unexpected thought popped into my head. A thought about horse tracks.

"Remember those horse tracks we saw on that road beside the ranch?" I said.

"What about 'em?" His black eyes searched my face.

"Seems strange to me that the thief would put Soapsuds in the trailer, then stop, take the horse out, put it back in the trailer, turn around, and then drive back down the way he'd come."

"Mmmm." He popped a stick of gum into his mouth. He seemed lost in thought. You can usually tell when a boy's thinking. It looks like it might be painful for him. I wondered if Leo and I were thinking the same thing.

At once his face brightened. *"That's it!"* he exclaimed.

"That no-good horse thief didn't put Soapsuds back in the trailer. He's still on the ranch somewhere."

"Exactly!" I said. "He had to hide Soapsuds—and Daddy—somewhere no one'd ever think to look for them."

"There's plenty of rugged country out there," he added. "Plenty of hidin' places." He scratched his head. "But I don't get why the thief didn't jest hightail it with that horse."

"It's not Soapsuds he wants. It's the ransom money."

Leo's face brightened. "You're right, gal!"

I said, "We've gotta go back to the ranch. Maybe there're still some tracks left we can follow."

Leo looked uncertain. "Yeah, but. . . ."

"But what?"

"What about that wolf?"

I grabbed his arm and looked him in the eye. "Leo, it's our only chance to find Daddy and Soapsuds." I glanced out the window. "We've gotta hurry, though. It'll be dark soon."

He nodded and answered, "OK. I'm willin'." At that moment I knew Leo to be my true friend.

I sliced some bread and took two apples for us, wrapping it all in newspaper. I took the bandanna from my hand and washed off the blood. I examined the cut. It didn't look too bad, but my hand felt stiff and sore. We went out the door, and I locked it behind us.

Outside I looked at the sky. The day was wearing out.

As usual, Leo insisted on steering the bike. He gripped the handlebars and let out a whoop. "Git on there, ol'

Paint! We got some ridin' to do. *Git along!*"

Sitting on the crossbar, I thought about Mama standing in line looking for work. What if she didn't get a job after all? What if I didn't find Daddy? Would we have to return to Liberal, Kansas and live with those frightful relations?

I just couldn't let that happen. I *had* to find Daddy!

Near the ranch we looked up the road and saw Frank's car coming our way. I yanked on Leo's shirt and he steered us to a place behind a thick mound of brush. The old Ford threw up clouds of dust as it rattled by.

"Let's go back where the tire tracks ended and look for hoofprints off the road," I suggested. "They must've either ridden Soapsuds or taken him through the thicket on foot."

I started for the side road, but Leo stopped me.

"Wait," he said. "We gotta have a horse."

"A *horse?*"

"Ain't enough light left to go on foot," he explained. "We could take one of Mr. Rogers' horses."

Taking a horse, even for a good reason, would be stealing, wouldn't it? I'd be no better than that scoundrel Joe Beck.

I shook my head. "That's stealing, Leo."

"Stealin' is takin' and not returnin'," Leo answered, shaking his head. "This's like borrowin'."

"Borrowing without asking permission," I corrected. I studied his face. I didn't see evil intentions there. I saw, instead, a friend out to help me find my father.

"Well," I said, "OK, but we've gotta leave a note and

we've gotta have the horse back quick."

We hid my bike behind some brush near Mr. Rogers' house. In the stable Leo picked a large chestnut quarter horse.

"This one's surefooted," my friend explained as he fitted a bit into the horse's mouth and pulled the crownpiece over its ears. "There. We'll go bareback. Be less trouble."

I found a stub of a pencil and I jotted a note to Frank on the back of Leo's awful handbill. I told Frank about borrowing the horse, noting that we'd have it back before dark, and laid it on a shelf in the stable.

Leo used a box to mount up and then gave me a hand and pulled me up behind him. I hadn't been on many horses in my life, and I felt uneasy being on this one. For one thing, it looked a long way to the ground. It didn't help any that we were "borrowing" the animal.

Leo trotted the horse off the ranch and down the side road. I clung to my friend's waist for fear of bouncing off. Leo made a clicking sound with his mouth and the horse started galloping. Even though the horse's gait became smoother, I felt I might just fly off behind.

"*Whoa!*" I yelled at Leo. I didn't figure the horse would pay me any mind.

"Gotta hurry," Leo explained. "Be dark pretty soon."

I gripped Leo tighter and shut my eyes.

Soon we reached the place where the tire tracks had ended. It would be slower going now because off the road the rugged land was covered with dense brush.

The horse stepped agilely through the wilderness. I dodged the low branches and swiped away cobwebs that swung down in our faces. White birds flew up like an explosion of sparks. Bugs fluttered into us. Every once in a while I heard creatures dart across the ground. Snakes? Lizards?

"Can't see no tracks from way up here," Leo complained. He swung to the ground. "Stay there," he said.

Leo led the horse, with me clinging to its mane, through the rough brush. I handed Leo his share of the bread and apples. As we went, a thousand thoughts coursed through my mind. Would Daddy be all right? What if we bumped into the horse thief? What if we couldn't find Daddy?

"Hey, lookee here, gal," Leo cried out, "*hoofprints!* And a *foot*print. They came through here all right."

My heart pounded. Could Daddy and Soapsuds be just beyond the next clump of trees?

We plunged deeper into the thicket, dodging limbs and vines and scrubby brush that scratched our clothes. The horse poked steadily ahead.

After a while Leo halted. His hands on his hips, he stared into the brush in front of us.

He crouched down beside the horse, holding the reins. I slid off and squatted beside him.

"Leo, what—" I began, but he clamped his hand over my mouth.

"*Shhh!*" His face inches from mine, he whispered, "I thought I heard somethin' up ahead. We gotta be quiet."

Kneeling beside him, I held my breath and listened.

Nothing. Leo stood up and led the horse ahead. Then paused. Then a few more steps. Then he stopped again and listened. Still nothing.

We crept on through the brush. Above, the sky changed to amber, then became purplish. Bright stars already twinkled in the heavens. The silence surrounding us felt thick and heavy.

An owl hooted and I jumped.

"Shhh!" Leo warned.

Then something did move ahead of us. I saw a branch bend and heard the sound of a foot stepping on dry brush.

Leo reached back, grabbed my shirt sleeve, and twisted it. He turned to me, his face pale with fright.

But this was no time for fear. It might be Daddy out there, and Soapsuds too. I just had to find them. I didn't care what nasty horse thief saw me. Only boldness counted now.

"Jessie!" Leo cried as I charged past him.

I hadn't taken two steps when I discovered the cause of his fear.

I stood face to face with a wolf!

Chapter 10

My mouth went dry. Sweat broke out on my forehead and neck. My heart seemed to rise up into my throat. I wanted to run, but my legs wouldn't budge.

In that dusky wood, the wolf's yellow eyes glistened. It growled and its pointed teeth glowed white.

Behind me Leo croaked, "D-don't move, gal."

I found my voice. "I *can't* move," I whispered back.

The wolf seemed to have all the patience in the world. It stood its ground, eyes fastened on me. It growled again and bared those long, white teeth. Teeth that could rip through clothes and skin. Teeth that could kill.

Staring at the creature, I prayed silently, *Father, please help us! Protect us from this . . . this beast!*

I inched backward, but the wolf seemed to sense my fear. Its growl grew more fierce. It took an abrupt step forward and a chill shook me.

"What'll we do?" I asked Leo.

"M-m-maybe it'll j-just go away," he stammered.

I glanced back. Leo stood with his eyes clamped shut, his whole body quivering. The rope he always wore attached to his belt quivered too.

Looking again at the wolf, I wondered if he was hungry and if we looked like dinner. I recalled the hungry look in the eyes of a neighbor's dog back in Oklahoma. The poor thing always looked half starved. Then I remembered how the dog's owners kept it tied up and how it always used to get the rope tangled around things in the yard.

The idea pounced on me like some wild animal. *The rope!* Of course, Leo's rope!

I reached back and grasped Leo's coiled rope. I yanked it and Leo whimpered.

"Give me the rope," I told him.

"The rope? F-f-for what?"

My eyes still on the wolf, I said, "I want to practice my lassoing." My voice sounded calm, masking the quaking fear that filled me.

"What!" he exclaimed.

"I'm gonna lasso that wolf," I said quietly.

"P-please don't throw that rope anywhere near that animal," Leo begged. "It'll kill us!"

"Give me the rope," I repeated.

"T-tell me what you're gonna do first."

With my eyes trained on the wolf, I said, "I'm gonna lasso it and then run and hope it gets tangled up in these trees and brush."

"That's crazy!" Leo gasped.

"Give me the rope," I said again. "Hurry." I looked back just long enough to see Leo, his face still full of fear, appear to be mulling over what I'd said. Then, as if he'd made up his mind about something, he nodded slightly to himself and cleared his throat.

"Move over, gal," he said. "I'll do it."

I frowned at him.

"I don't plan to risk my neck on your two lassoin' lessons. If you miss, we're dead."

I moved. His hands shaking, Leo let go of the horse's reins and slowly untied the leather thong holding the rope to his belt. The horse snorted, tossed its head, and backed up.

The wolf took another step forward and growled. The sound sank deep into the thicket. The horse reared and neighed. Then it turned and lit out.

Bad as it seemed, I couldn't worry about the horse running off. I had my mind set on the wolf. And on Leo lassoing it.

"You can do it, Leo," I whispered to encourage him. "Throw it right around its neck."

Leo made a lasso and swung it up over his head. The wolf didn't like that. It crept forward. My friend let the lasso fall to his feet.

Leo's teeth rattled as his whole body shook. "J-Jessie, maybe we should just run."

"We can't outrun a wolf," I whispered. "You can do it, Leo. Once you throw the lasso, give me the rope and run to the left, through the thicket. And don't stop."

He didn't answer. I hoped he'd do like I said. If he didn't, we might both get mauled by this creature.

He twirled the lasso again, careful to keep it low and away from the branches. The wolf stepped forward, baring its teeth. Its yellow eyes glowed. I wanted to run myself, but I knew that would be foolish. The wolf would be on me in a flash.

"H-here goes," Leo said. "Get ready."

I held my breath and watched him let go of the lasso. It looped through the air and landed—right around the wolf's neck! The animal lurched and its yellow eyes exploded with hatred.

"Run!" Leo screamed.

I grabbed the coiled rope as Leo plunged into the thicket to our left. I dashed right just as the wolf leaped forward, his growl tearing through the night. I zigzagged through the brush and trees, letting out the rest of the rope as I ran. I heard the wolf's ferocious growling, but I didn't look back.

When I reached the end of the rope, I pulled tight and tied it around one of the slender trees near me.

I could hear the wolf struggling. I prayed he was tangled up good.

Leo came tramping through the brush near me.

"Leo!" I sang out. "Are you OK?"

His voice came back surprised, as if amazed I'd outlived this stupid stunt. "Y-y-yep. What about you?"

From just a few feet away the wolf howled up a storm.

"Let's get outta here!" I said.

Scrambling through the brush, we put distance between us and the wolf.

Finally, we worked our way back out to the side road. I sighed, relieved, but I grew troubled pretty quick.

The chestnut horse was nowhere in sight.

"Where's that horse?" I said, looking up and down the dirt road.

"Don't know," he admitted.

"We've *gotta* find it," I cried. "Frank may be back by now. The note said before dark. He'll call the sheriff if we don't return that horse soon."

We ran down the road. The sound of our footsteps pierced the quiet dusk.

Frank's awful words had unrightly branded my father a horse thief. But now those words also pointed at me. Jessie Land, horse thief. I pictured all sorts of things. Frank coming across the note. The sheriff ready to handcuff me. Mama's eyes full of shame and disappointment. Mrs. Jackman nodding like she knew all along I'd only come to trouble. Maybe they were all crazy thoughts, but I couldn't squeeze them out of my head.

We reached the ranch, out of breath, tired. Still no sign of the horse. As I retrieved my bicycle from its hiding place, I glanced over at the stable. Frank's car was back!

"Leo—" I began. I was about to say, "We might as well face up to Frank and tell him the horse ran off." But Leo's hand on my arm stopped me.

"We'd best git out of here, gal," Leo whispered, nodding at the stable.

Somehow his words at that moment made sense. I decided not to listen to my conscience.

This time I made Leo sit on the crossbar. I pedaled that bike like mad. Like a guilty person bent on escape.

It was dark when I dropped Leo off at the migrant camp. I rode quickly home. Mama would be worried sick. First Daddy and now me missing. But when I got to the apartment, the door was still locked. Inside, I saw Mama hadn't been home yet.

Mama, where are you? I wondered, though I felt some relief. How could I tell her that her very own daughter had stolen a horse?

I gulped down a glass of water, undressed, and collapsed on the couch. My body ached and a thousand thoughts swirled in my head. I shut my eyes, hoping my brain would stop working. Before I fell asleep, I lay there for the longest time, remembering and worrying.

And wondering. *What about horses? Does God watch over missing horses too?*

Chapter 11

When I woke up the next morning, I felt groggy and confused. I kept my eyes closed and pictured our farm back in southeast Oklahoma. It was a nice little place before the drought. Each morning the sky sparkled blue and cloudless. The air smelled fresh. Birds chattered outside my window.

But the awful truth of the past day crashed on top of me when I opened my eyes. I shoved the sheet covering me off the sofa and glanced around. Where was Mama?

I got up and went to the dining room table. On a scrap of paper I found a note in Mama's handwriting.

Jessie,

The Lord has blessed us. I found a Job with Mr. Dudley, a lawyer. I had to help him last night with some filing and by the time I got home you were already asleep. I didn't have the Heart to wake you. I left a little early for Work this morning. You will have to make your own meals today. I Prayed for your daddy, so stay close to Home in case someone brings word about him. Or in case he comes Home himself! I'll be back by about 6 o'clock tonight.

Love,
Mama

I clutched the note and thought about all the things Mama didn't even know. About all that had happened yesterday. Leo and me tracking the thief and losing the chestnut horse. I recalled with a chill the yellow eyes of the wolf. But I'd face that creature again if it would bring back that horse.

I reread the note and wondered how my staying home would help Daddy. Those interested in finding him just wanted to stick him behind bars. Only I wanted to prove him innocent. How could I do that from this apartment?

Having no answer to that, I returned to the sofa, folded up the sheet, and straightened the cushions. I made myself a breakfast of day-old biscuits and jam. As little as I'd eaten yesterday, I could hardly choke them down. If only Daddy would come back, then I'd eat plenty!

I put on my overalls and tugged on my stiff, heavy shoes. Then I cleaned up and brushed my short, cropped hair. Looking into the mirror, I just saw a red-haired girl with brown eyes, a small nose, and a determined chin. I didn't really look like a horse thief. Or the daughter of one either. I knelt down by the sofa and said my prayers. I prayed for Daddy's safe return. I prayed he'd be proved innocent. I prayed that Soapsuds and the quarter horse would turn up and that Daddy could keep his job with Will Rogers. And I prayed for forgiveness for taking and losing that horse.

Just as I said "Amen," I heard automobile tires screeching outside. I got up and went to the window in Mama and Daddy's tiny bedroom. Peeking out, I saw a familiar black convertible. Then a familiar battered hat.

Frank Dubois!

He was coming to get me sure enough! I only glimpsed his red face, but it didn't take much to figure him to be angry. He'd found my note. Proof enough that I was a no-good horse thief.

I heard a knock at the front door! What should I do? If I went to the door, he would surely cart me off to the sheriff and to jail.

The knocking at the door grew fierce. Glancing at the window, I saw the only way out. Back at the front door, Frank called out something.

I opened the window and climbed out. Just like a thief. This proved it. I was sneaking out the window and fleeing like a true villain.

I raced for my bicycle. Then I pushed off and hopped on. I pedaled like never before. I pedaled harder than I had yesterday when Leo and I fled that awful Joe Beck. Harder than last night when I first became a horse thief. The wooden rear tire kept skidding. At that moment I hated that homemade bicycle. But I don't suppose even the red beauty in Hopper's store would have suited me. I wanted *speed.*

I pedaled and prayed. Prayed for forgiveness and prayed to go faster. Maybe later I'd pray for forgiveness for praying for speed. But now I just wanted to get far, far away.

I stayed on the main street. Before long I rattled along at a good clip. Gasping for air, I kept looking back, watching for Frank's car. I expected it any minute.

I guess I didn't pay enough attention to the street. After glancing over my shoulder again, I turned back to watch in horror as my front tire headed straight for a large, round rock. I jerked the handlebars to the left. Too late. I hit the rock head on.

Blam!

My bike collapsed like a heap of dried sticks. I tumbled down and cartwheeled beside the street.

Ooof!

For a moment I couldn't move. I just lay there trying to catch my breath. Then my eyes opened and I stared at my poor, wrecked bicycle. The rear wooden tire had split in two. The pipe frame looked bent.

"I'm sorry, Daddy," I said aloud.

I got up, brushed myself off, and glanced back. Frank's car appeared on the street. It headed right for me!

Leaving the ruins of my bike behind, I tore off down the street. Tires screeched and a car door slammed.

"Hey, you! Hey, Jessie Land! Come back here!"

He'd seen me! He stood in front of his car, waving his arms. I kept running, just like I had pedaled—as hard as I could. Behind me Frank yelled, *"Hey, wait up! I want a word with you!"*

I looked back and saw him hop in his car. I ran harder. I had to get out of there. And fast.

I saw my chance. If I dashed across the street and tore down the hill, Frank might not find me. But there were too many cars rushing up and down the street. To run across it now would be foolish. Maybe deadly.

Still, Frank kept coming. I had to go now!

Taking a deep breath, I bolted into the busy street. A horn bellowed at me.

Ahhhhh-oooooooo-gggaaaaa!

I got safely to the middle of the street. Then I ran up the middle between the flow of cars. Folks yelled at me something fierce. At just the right moment I plunged on across. Horns blared. Tires squealed. But I reached the other side in one piece.

As I stopped to catch my breath, I heard a familiar voice call out to me.

"You, girl, come here," the voice barked. "Right this minute!"

I glanced around. The sheriff! He had stopped his car right in the middle of the street. He stood on the running board of his vehicle and waved me toward him with a hand holding an orange. *Dear Lord, what did he want?* A fearful question shot into my brain. *Had Frank already told him about the missing quarter horse? Did the sheriff plan to take me to jail?*

Instead of obeying his command, I darted around a building and dived headlong down a grassy hill. I tumbled down the slope, rolling over and over. When I landed on level ground, I just lay there, trying to get my dizzy head to stop spinning.

My goodness! The life of a fugitive was nothing to boast about.

Jumping to my feet, I took off down another street. Then it struck me that I had no idea where I was running to. At the end of the block, I stopped again, gasping for air.

No one yelled at me. I'd lost Frank and the sheriff, I felt pretty sure. *So now, Jessie Land,* I asked myself, *where will you go?* The answer came as I watched a boy tugging at a woman's skirts. "Mama," he said, "let's go."

Mama!

She'd know what to do. Even though I'd done a heap of wrong, she'd forgive me. She'd understand.

Now I had to find that Mr. Dudley's law office. I had no idea where it might be, so I started asking folks walking along the street. They all shook their heads. When I came to a print shop, I went in and asked the ink-stained man inside. He shoved his spectacles up on his forehead and scratched his nose, leaving a black smudge. His moustache twitched as he considered my question.

Finally, he said, "Go over two blocks to High Street. I think his office is to your left another block or so. I printed some business cards for him not long ago."

I thanked him and left. Imagine coming home every night looking like you swam in an ink well!

I raced up the two blocks, still watchful for the sheriff and Frank. When I reached High Street, I slowed. I was plenty sick of running, so I turned left and, walking along, studied the storefronts.

Then I spotted it. From across the street I could make out his sign in the plate glass window. It read:

J. Randolph Dudley, Attorney-at-Law

I crossed High Street and glanced in the office. I could see someone through the glass. Someone in a white blouse and a dark skirt. *Mama!* At once, I felt relieved. I smiled as I saw her leaning over a desk. She looked so lovely.

I crossed the street, and just as I was about to go in the door a hand came from nowhere, grabbed my shoulder, and spun me around. Before my eyes even settled on him, his voice made me gasp.

"Well, well, just the little squirt I've been lookin' for."

His painful-looking grin sank into me like a hook. I stared right into the awful face of Joe Beck.

Chapter 12

I saw my frightened face reflected in Beck's sunglasses. He held my arm tight, but even if he'd let go I would have been too scared to move. I knew Joe Beck meant business.

He sneered, "You owe me for a window, squirt."

Window! Suddenly I remembered Mama back in the window. I swung around and started to scream, but his arm corralled me and his hand, smelling of dust and sweat, clamped tight over my mouth.

I jerked right and left, shaking my head and kicking my legs, hoping someone would see me. But not a soul came down this street. Beck tightened his grip on me and began pulling me away. I forced my mouth open and sunk my teeth as deep as I could into the fleshy part of his palm.

"Yeeeoooowwwwww!" he cried out, snatching his hand away.

I yelled, *"Mama! Help me, Mama!"*

But his injured hand flew back to my mouth, muffling my cry. This time I could scarcely breathe.

"I'll fix you, you little squirt!" he barked.

Suddenly, he ripped my feet from the ground and started carrying me. My feet flailed in the air, trying to kick him, or at least trying to find the ground again. His hand covered my nose and my mouth so tight that I grew dizzy and faint.

We moved toward a car parked a few feet away. The green car with yellow, spoked wheels. I knew I'd be thrown into that vehicle and hustled away to certain doom.

I kept struggling. I stiffened my body and tried to drag my feet. I jerked around as best I could with my arms locked under his.

"Come on, come on," the villain grunted, unsatisfied with the slow progress he was making toward his car.

Dear Lord, help me, I prayed.

Beside the car, he let loose of my mouth so he could yank open the driver's door. I gasped for air then tried to scream. It came out a mere gurgle. I managed to pull one arm free and I swung my fist at the brute. He batted it away like he would a pesky housefly.

Then a miracle happened. Over Beck's shoulder I spied Leo Little Wolf ambling up the street.

Leo! Dear, dear Leo. He occupied himself twirling a lasso.

Beck grunted, "Get in there, squirt, *now!*"

As he leaned slightly back to gather momentum for a final shove, I yelled, *"Leo! Help! Help!"*

My friend looked up and spotted me. Beck butted his hands against me, shoving me into the car. I lay sprawled on the front seat. My legs dangled outside.

Leo shrieked, "I'm a-comin', gal!"

Surprised, Beck lurched around. In that instant I managed to pull up one leg. My foot shot out, slamming my shoe into the villain's shin.

Groaning, Beck hopped back, off balance. Then swooping over his head and shoulders came Leo's lasso, expertly thrown.

"Got ya, you outlaw!" Leo yelled.

With Beck struggling against the rope, I slid across the seat and out the car door.

Leo leaped behind him and yanked the man's hat down, knocking his sunglasses off. Beck's eyes fixed on me. They surprised me. I expected beady, black, snake eyes, but these were brilliant blue. This was no mere man. This was a vile, suit-wearing serpent with a baby's eyes.

Leo grabbed my hand and pulled me away. I wanted to run for Mr. Dudley's office. But Leo's strong arm kept dragging me the other direction.

We fled as Beck struggled with the lasso and roared after us, *"I'll get you!"*

We raced down an alley, then crossed a busy street. It seemed I'd spent my whole life running from one man or another, every one of them out to do me ill. I wanted to sit down and catch my breath, but Leo kept pulling me along. When we reached an alley heaped with broken crates and trash barrels, Leo ducked into it and we collapsed together on the ground. Across the street I saw Hopper's store.

For a time we sat still, gasping for air. When I could talk, I said, "Thank goodness you happened by, Leo."

"Yeah, I reckon so," he agreed, breathing heavily and running his plump hand through his wild, black hair. "But I'm runnin' outta rope gettin' us out of scrapes."

"How in the world did you happen to be on that street?" I asked.

His dark eyes settled on me. Sweat trickled down his pudgy, brown cheeks. "I come by your apartment. The door was unlocked, so I went on in."

Uh-oh. I'd left it unlocked when I'd fled from Frank.

"I found your ma's note," he continued, "so I headed for Mr. Dudley's office to see if I could find you."

"Thank the Lord," I said, sighing in relief that Leo'd come along when he did.

"So now where do we go?"

"We can't go back to see Mama," I said, "not with that Beck around."

"What about the ranch?" Leo offered. "We could search for the quarter horse."

"Not with the sheriff and Frank watching for us we can't. What we need," I began, looking past Leo, "is someone we can trust. A grown-up. Someone who could talk to the sheriff and convince him that Joe Beck's the true horse thief, not Daddy. Someone the sheriff would believe."

"Yeah," Leo said. "But who might that be?"

My eyes settled on the front of the store across the street. I saw the red bicycle in the window and beyond that I saw Mr. Hopper speaking to a customer.

Of course! Mr. Hopper!

I yanked Leo up by the hand. "Come on."

"Where to?"

I remembered how we'd hidden from Beck in Hopper's store just yesterday. "To a safe place," I said. Safe, yes—maybe the one safe place in town.

We peeked out the entrance of the alley. People filled the street, but there was no sign of Beck, no sign of Frank, no sign of the sheriff. We raced across the street and I stopped outside the door to Hopper's store.

"Here?" Leo huffed. "Why here?"

"Mr. Hopper's a person we can trust," I said.

Leo started to speak, but his words were lost in the tinkling of the bell as I opened the front door. He followed me inside.

Mr. Hopper looked up from his customer. Seeing us, he frowned slightly. But at once the frown became a smile. I'd been right. Mr. Hopper would help us.

Leo and I walked around in the store. I stopped at the red bike, ran my fingers over its shiny fender. All the trouble I'd had lately and still I had a powerful urge to own this bike. Leo stayed right with me, glancing around and fidgeting, ready to bolt any second.

He tugged at my sleeve and whispered, "Gal, let's git outta here. I don't think—"

"Thank you, Miss West," I heard Mr. Hopper say. "I'll send in your order this afternoon. It should be shipped next week."

I grabbed Leo's arm and pulled him after me, toward the back of the store where Mr. Hopper stood writing on a pad beside the cash register. The front door tinkled as the customer left.

Mr. Hopper looked up. A friendly smile spread across his face. His eyes brightened like he was glad to see me!

"Good morning, Jessie Land," he said. Leo stood off a ways. I guessed Mr. Hopper didn't notice him because he didn't speak to my friend.

"Morning, Mr. Hopper," I said. Then my throat went dry. How on earth could I tell him all I needed to?

"What can I do for you?" Mr. Hopper asked.

I hesitated, wet my lips, and swallowed. Then I began, "Well, sir, I wondered if you could . . . well, help us."

Mr. Hopper's face turned serious as he studied me. The store became deadly silent. I felt like a bug in a jar.

"Yes?" came Mr. Hopper's reply.

Leo nudged me. I stepped away from him. I didn't need prodding by anyone. Especially by someone too afraid to speak himself. Then I did it. I just opened my mouth and it all came out, the whole story. Even the part about the ransom note in Daddy's handwriting and about Leo and me taking and losing the quarter horse. Now Mr. Hopper knew more than even Mama did.

As I spoke, his eyes widened. He stuck his hands in his pockets and jingled his change. He looked from me to Leo.

Finally, he said, "That's quite a story."

I nodded.

Then he said, "What about your mother? Does she know about all of this?"

I shook my head. "I was about to tell her, but Joe Beck nearly caught me this morning across the street from where she's working. We can't go back there now. He might be waiting."

"I see," he replied, looking worriedly at the counter in front of him. He jingled the coins ever so fiercely now. "And this Jim Beck—he's the horse thief, you say?"

"*Joe* Beck. Yes, sir," I replied.

"Well, let me think."

I waited. Leo fidgeted beside me, impatient, ready to go.

Finally, Mr. Hopper cleared his throat and said, "I suppose I could talk to the sheriff. Do you think that might help?"

Relief flooded through me. I wanted to leap into his arms and give him a big hug. But of course I didn't. I hardly knew the man.

Instead, I smiled and said, "Yes, sir. I think that would help quite a bit, coming from you."

He thought a moment, then excused himself and went into the back room. He came back at once.

"You'd best wait somewhere until I get back," he said. "Is there a place you could go?"

Go? I took that to mean we shouldn't go with him, and we couldn't wait here in the store. I looked at Leo. His dark eyes shone like bright stones. What in the world was he thinking?

Turning back to Mr. Hopper, I told him, "We'll wait in the alley across the street."

"All right," he said. "I'll be back as soon as I can. You stay put, even if it takes a while. All right?"

I nodded and we went out the front door together, the bell tinkling as the door closed behind us. Mr. Hopper put up a sign: BE BACK SOON. Then he locked the door and headed up the street toward the sheriff's office. Leo and I watched him go.

As we settled in our hiding place in the alley, I thought, *Everything depends on Mr. Hopper now. Absolutely everything.*

* * *

I don't know how long we waited in that alley. It seemed like hours. My mind felt tense and tight like an over-wound watch. Leo kept getting up and peering out at the street. Twice he even went and stood on the sidewalk until I rushed out and dragged him back.

"Maybe the sheriff was out," Leo said after a while.

I kept still. More time passed and I thought about Mama. Did she worry as she worked in Mr. Dudley's office? Or did she think Daddy might've made his way home and that Soapsuds would turn up and things would be all right?

And what about Daddy? Was he hurt? Where was he?

I heard a car. Why that made my heart race I couldn't really say. Mr. Hopper had left on foot. He'd like as not return that way, unless the sheriff believed him and the two of them were coming back in the sheriff's car to talk to us.

Just then a dark car pulled up in front of the alley, blocking our view of the store. The driver's door swung open.

Leo spoke the words before me. "Uh-oh."

I stared into the smiling face of Joe Beck. An icy chill rained inside me. The man's smile curled on his lips. In his fist, he clutched a pistol, aimed right at me and Leo.

"Well, well, if it isn't Miss Jessie Land and her faithful sidekick," he said. For some reason, his very words terrified me.

"Hopper's a no-good rat," Leo spat. "He double-crossed us good!"

"No!" I insisted. "He just got waylaid is all."

I glanced behind us. The alley ended at a tall fence.

"No use looking back that way," Beck said with a sneer. "You squirts ain't escaping from me this time."

Chapter 13

He had us. Beck waved his gun and we marched to the car. We climbed in, Leo first, then me.

Beck got in after us and warned, "Stay put and keep your traps shut." Then he started the car, stomped on the gas pedal, and tore down the street. I glanced back. What was keeping Mr. Hopper and the sheriff?

We drove out of town, turning down a rutted dirt road. We bounced around in that seat something awful. Beck didn't seem to care. He raced down the road with a fury.

After a while we reached a deserted farm. Boards covered the windows and doors of the peeling, ramshackle farmhouse. The pens held no livestock. A rusted car missing its doors and tires sat in a field of weeds like an old animal carcass. Beside it I spied a faded red horse trailer.

Horse trailer! I perked up. Beck swung the car past the trailer, then backed up to it. He shut off the engine.

"Ever hook up a trailer, squirt?" he asked me.

Suddenly irritated, I snapped at him, "I'm no fonder of the word "squirt" now than I was the first time you called me that."

He pulled the gun from his pocket and snarled, "I asked you if you ever hooked up a trailer."

My fear of the man returned and I shook my head.

"Well, you're gonna learn. Both of you, get out of the car. Go on!"

Leo opened his door and we slid out. I glanced around. It might've been the perfect time to escape, but the nearest building, the barn, stood quite a ways off.

"I know what you're thinking," Beck said. "Forget it. You try running, you'll be plenty sorry. Believe me."

I believed him. So did Leo. Neither of us ran.

Beck grabbed a coiled rope from the back seat. Leo's rope! Then he led us toward the back of the car.

"Lift up the tongue of that trailer and fit it down on the hitch," he ordered.

Leo and I struggled with the heavy trailer tongue. Beck made no move to help.

Finally, we managed to hook the tongue onto the trailer hitch. Then Beck directed us to wrap the chain around the bumper. Leo finished the work by snapping a rusty lock onto the chain.

"OK, squirts, get on to the back of the trailer," Beck commanded, grinning and motioning with his gun.

As we walked past the side of the trailer, I glanced down. There, as if cut with a knife, I spied a large nick in one of the trailer's tires.

"*Look,* Leo!" I whispered, pointing to the tire.

Leo nodded and muttered, "He's the villain awright. But I got us a plan. Fall to the ground."

"But—"

"Just do it, gal."

Beck growled, "Get moving, you two, and be quiet about it."

I wanted to tell Leo to forget his foolish cowboy hero notions, but determination shone in his eyes. You can't easily talk sense once a boy's set his mind on something.

Near the back of the trailer I pretended to stumble though there wasn't a thing to stumble over. I plunged to the dirt.

Leo yelled, *"Yah!"*

When I turned to look, Beck had Leo by the shirt collar. Leo squirmed like a wild pig.

So much for that plan.

Beck smiled his painful-looking smile and ordered me into the trailer. As I climbed in, he tied Leo's hands behind his back.

"Good thing you threw this rope at me this morning, squirt," Beck snapped. "It's coming in handy now."

"Ow!" cried Leo. "You got it too tight!"

When Beck was finished, he shoved my friend into the trailer. Leo sprawled beside me.

"All right, squirt, now you," Beck said to me.

Much as I didn't want to go near him, I obeyed. He tied my hands with the other end of the rope. As he pulled the knot tight, I grew angry.

"You'll be sorry you interfered with Jessie Land," I declared.

"I've been sorry since I laid eyes on you," he grumbled. Then he shoved me deep into the trailer and slammed the door shut.

Trapped. And in complete darkness. A blackness crept through me at that moment. Fear rattled me and I felt like I couldn't breathe. Gasping, I fretted, *what's to become of us? There's no escape. I'll never help Daddy now.*

I heard the car start. The trailer jerked forward and I crashed to the floor. Leo rolled into me.

"Leo, how will we ever get out of here?" I whined.

"Jest work on your bindin's, gal," he answered. I could hear him pulling at the knotted ropes securing his hands.

The trailer rocked along the bumpy road. Inside, it smelled of hay and old wood and horses. I tried to think how I might get free.

I rolled back to the door, getting a mouthful of dusty hay for my trouble. I spit it out and kicked the door with all my strength. No use. Beck had bolted it shut from the outside. Not even a grown man could've kicked it open.

When I rolled back to Leo, I felt him jerking one way, then another. Scooting up and down and around. He had a knack for ropes. If anyone could get untied, it was Leo.

I gave it a try myself. I tugged and twisted my arms, pulling one way, then another. Nothing. Squirming didn't help. Nothing did.

"Joe Beck might not know much," I complained, "but he knows his knots. I'll give him that."

"Ain't no such thing as a knot that you can't untie," Leo replied.

After a while I got tired of twisting and tugging and

stretching. I lay in a heap on the trailer floor. Leo kept after it though. I could hear him in the dark as we rocked along. Every now and then he'd bump into me. He just kept after that rope.

Where were we headed? What were Beck's intentions? Would I ever see Daddy again? Or Mama? The unanswered questions, the darkness, the closeness all spooked me. To comfort myself, I started to sing.

"Just as I am, Thou wilt receive,
Wilt welcome, pardon, cleanse, relieve;
Because Thy promise I believe,
O Lamb of God, I come! I come!"

At once I felt relief. God calmed my heart. Just as He had when I came to California. He kept me safe that whole perilous journey. Now I needed His help again. I needed one of God's mighty angels to swoop down right now and knock Joe Beck's block off.

Immediately I felt sorry for that harsh thought. *Forgive me, Lord!* I just needed to get the ropes off. I shouldn't wish uncharitable treatment on anyone, even a rotten snake like Joe Beck.

I had a long time for these kinds of thoughts. Then I felt the car slow down.

As it came to a stop, I discovered a tiny crack in the side of the trailer. A ray of light filtered inside. Springing to my feet, I went to the crack and tried peering out. I saw a narrow sliver of blue sky and a narrower sliver of dry brush. Nothing else.

The car door slammed shut. I heard Beck's heels crunch on the ground outside. Then—

Blam! Blam! Blam! Blam!

My heart nearly stopped at the racket.

"Havin' fun in there, squirts?" Beck called out. "Well, enjoy yourselves. You'll be there a good long while. Till dark leastwise."

I heard him walk off.

I crossed over to Leo. He still worked away on his rope. He amazed me the way he kept after a thing like that till he got it licked.

Plopping down beside him, I considered our problem. We couldn't get loose from the ropes. We couldn't get out of the trailer. All of a sudden Leo nudged me. In that tiny sliver of light I could see both of his arms.

"Leo!" I cried. "You're free!"

His hand came up to my mouth. "Shhhh. He might hear."

I shook my head. "I heard him tromp off into the brush somewhere."

"He'll be back. I gotta get you loose. When he opens that door next time, we'll jump out and surprise him good."

Much as I feared Beck, it seemed like the only plan. I didn't intend to stay locked inside this dark, hot, smelly trailer forever.

Leo worked at the rope holding my hands for quite a while. He complained, "You're tied tighter'n I was."

"No wonder I couldn't get loose," I said, not admitting that I hadn't tried as hard as he had to free myself.

"Turn your back to that light," he suggested. "Maybe it'll help."

As he struggled with the rope, I said, "Leo, you're wrong about Mr. Hopper. He didn't double-cross us."

"Who else knew we were waitin' in that alley?" he replied.

"You went out in the street twice," I reminded him. "Beck must've seen you."

"Well, maybe. Hold still, willya?"

"He's always been nice to me," I said, recalling Mr. Hopper's face the day I visited the store, that day those rude boys laughed at my clothes and my bike. When was that? Goodness, just yesterday morning. It seemed ages ago.

* * *

Hours passed. I grew hungry. Leo had long before freed my hands, but I felt like a caged animal locked in that trailer. The precious sliver of light disappeared. It was night.

Then I heard footsteps tramping through dry leaves and brush.

I heard a low voice. Joe Beck's for sure. But maybe another too. Would a whole gang of thieves descend on us now?

"Get back over there," Leo said.

"But—"

He leaned close and whispered, "I'll stand by the door and spring out at him. You jump out after me and run. Maybe I can get his gun."

I shook my head frantically. "*No,* Leo! Don't—" But I knew I must hush or we'd be in a bigger mess.

I heard the bolt on the door slide. Then, just as the door cracked, Leo crashed against it. *"Yah!"*

I made out a shape in the darkness. Beck, I thought, springing backward. I rushed to the door to jump out. But something hard pressed against me, stopping me short.

"Back inside, squirt," Beck ordered.

He had the *gun* on me! I obeyed.

"Yah! Yah! Yah!" shouted Leo.

A horse neighed.

Beck cried out, "You little brat!"

"Yah! Yah!"

I made out Leo running in circles around Beck. The villain reached out and gave Leo a hard shove. My friend skidded down to the ground.

"Leo!" I cried out.

Before Beck could grab him, Leo shot back to his feet and yelled, *"I'm goin' for help, gal!"* I didn't see him, but I heard him run off.

"Come back here!" Beck shouted, but Leo was gone. No one could match him for speed.

I sighed in relief. Leo had escaped.

Beck turned to me. I saw his outline in the moonlight. I backed up, holding my hands behind me.

I stared out the trailer door as Beck fiddled with a wooden plank. Then I could make out the shape of a horse. Soapsuds? The horse snorted as he stepped reluctantly up the wooden ramp into the trailer. His smell filled the trailer.

Then Beck pushed something else inside. A person! Someone gagged and bound groaned and slumped to the floor beside the horse. I studied the shape. A man. What with the moon and bright stars shining outside, I could make out the man's bruised forehead and smudged cheek.

Not much to go on, but still I knew.

Daddy!

Chapter 14

A beam from Joe Beck's flashlight shot around inside the trailer. He climbed in just long enough to tie Soapsuds' lead to a metal ring on the side wall. I kept my arms behind my back.

My father lay slumped in a heap near the trailer door. Even in the dark I could tell that he'd been hurt pretty bad. He groaned. Beck aimed the light at him. The sight of his face took my breath away.

A dirty, white gag turned his mouth down grimly. Whiskers darkened his face around the gag. His dark brown hair hung limp over eyes that looked sunken and circled in black. He appeared beaten, defeated.

Daddy still wore what I'd last seen him in, including the blue shirt. Sure enough, one sleeve had been ripped, the cuff was missing. His muscular forearm looked badly scratched.

Beck jumped out of the trailer, turned, and shone the light in my face.

"Hey, Land," Beck growled, "you're gonna be keepin' company with your precious little girl."

Even with the light in my eyes I could make out Daddy

turning toward me. Beck slammed the door shut. Trapped again!

I stumbled toward Daddy. Then I threw my arms around him and hugged him hard. His hands still tied, he couldn't hug me back. Soapsuds neighed and stamped beside us, swaying as the trailer began bumping along.

"Mama and I've been so worried about you," I cried. "Everyone thinks you stole Soapsuds. Everyone's after you."

It struck me that these words probably didn't do much to ease his mind.

I let him go and struggled with the gag. After some time I worked it loose. Daddy's cry exploded in the trailer, *"My dear, sweet Jess!"*

"Daddy, lemme get your hands loose," I said.

I pulled at the rope, digging my fingertips into the tight knot.

As I worked at it, Daddy said, "I thought I'd never see you again, Jess."

It was the name he always used for me and it sounded splendid to my ears. As splendid as his warm, rich voice. Though now his voice seemed older and tired and weak.

As the trailer swayed, I continued to work on his bindings. Soapsuds snorted and stomped.

A long time passed. Then, unexpectedly, I felt the knot unravel and come apart.

"You're free!" I cried. At once his arms came around me. I hugged him and kissed his coarse cheek.

"Oh, Daddy, I've been looking for you since yesterday

morning," I told him. "Since Frank came and told me and Mama about you and Soapsuds disappearing." I told him everything, from first to last. Even about me and Leo losing that quarter horse. Then I asked, "What happened? How did you and Soapsuds get kidnapped?"

He sighed so deep it sent a shudder through him. Sitting close by, I felt it.

"I keep going over it in my mind," he said. "Trying to make sense of it all."

"Tell me."

"Well, Jess, you know I'd been working hard all day, and I was plumb tuckered out," he explained. "When it got dark, I decided to get some shuteye and then get up at first light. I hadn't been asleep long when the horses woke me."

"Was Frank there?" I asked.

"No, he went home at sundown, the way he usually does. It was just me. I got up and saw this car and horse trailer up at the stable. And this—this fella in dark glasses was leading Soapsuds out of his stall. Then someone came up behind me and clobbered me good. I never saw him."

"That scoundrel in sunglasses is Joe Beck," I explained. "But who hit you?"

"Don't know," Daddy said. "When I came to, there was just this Beck fella and he was putting me across Soapsuds' back. I got in a fight with him. Got my shirt tore and my arm scraped up some and another knock on the head for my trouble." He added, "Your mama'll be sore. My best shirt."

"Where did Beck have you hid?"

"At Mr. Rogers' cabin he's been building," he replied. "No one's been out there for days."

"The cabin!" I cried. "Leo and I knew you had to be somewhere on the ranch."

"Beck seemed to know a lot about the ranch," Daddy said bitterly.

"I'll bet he's the one who got you to write that ransom note."

Daddy sat in quiet for a moment. I figured the memory of writing that note stung plenty. Finally, he said, "Jess, he told me he had you and your mother locked up somewhere. Like a fool I believed him. Your mother's all right, isn't she?"

"She's fine. She found a job because we needed to pay the rent, and Frank wouldn't give Mama your pay."

"What?" I heard him breathe deep. He did that sometimes when something angered him. He paused, like he didn't want to say something harsh he might later regret. "Well, God bless her. Maybe the job kept her mind off this terrible mess."

"Daddy," I said suddenly, "how're we gonna escape?

"Well, we can't kick that door down," Daddy said. "I heard him bolt it shut."

Soapsuds snorted. Suddenly I got a crazy idea. "We can't knock it down, but maybe Soapsuds can."

"Soapsuds!"

"You've seen him kick," I reminded him. "Remember how when Mr. Rogers rubs his foreleg a certain way,

Soapsuds rears up and starts kicking?"

Daddy laughed. "Yes. A crazy idea for sure, Jess."

"Maybe crazy enough to work."

The trailer rocked over the rough road. I braced myself against the side and stood up. Daddy stood beside me and untied the rope securing the horse.

He asked, "You remember how Mr. Rogers rubbed him?"

"Yes, but watch out, Daddy."

"Don't worry about me. Go ahead."

I stooped in front of the horse and rubbed his foreleg just above the knee, preparing myself for the kick.

Nothing happened. I rubbed again, this time harder.

Still nothing.

"Jess, what's wrong?" Daddy asked.

"I don't know. It's not working."

"Which leg are you rubbing?"

Of course! I pictured Mr. Rogers rubbing Soapsuds' left leg. I'd been rubbing the right.

"Get ready," I told Daddy, then began rubbing the horse's left leg.

Soapsuds snorted. *Yes!* I rubbed harder. He neighed and tipped forward.

"Thatta girl!" Daddy cried. "Keep it up."

I kept rubbing. Finally, Soapsuds let go with a mighty backward kick. The whole trailer shook when his rear hooves crashed into the door.

"It bent the door some," Daddy sang out. "Let me check his hooves."

I had imagined one kick and the door would fly off, but this would take more work.

"He's OK," Daddy said. "But he can't do this too many times. I sure don't want him getting injured."

I stooped before the horse and rubbed furiously at his left foreleg. He snorted again and kicked. This time I didn't back away but kept after him.

Blam! Blam! Blam!

He kicked again and again, each jolt jarring the trailer. I wondered if Joe Beck felt it. Or heard it. Inside, the sound had been like thunderclaps.

"That's good!" Daddy yelled. "I think I can shove—"

Suddenly the trailer door swung back and collapsed. It hung loose from the trailer by the heavy bottom hinge and dragged on the dirt road behind us.

The car slowed.

"Get ready, Jess!" Daddy exclaimed.

Daddy grabbed the horse's lead, close to the halter.

The car stopped. Daddy quickly backed Soapsuds out of the trailer using the broken door like a ramp.

I heard a car door slam. Beck was coming!

Chapter 15

We jumped out of the trailer. One hand grasping mine and the other leading the horse, Daddy rushed us off into the darkness before Beck appeared. We ran a little ways, then Daddy leaped on Soapsuds' back and yanked me up behind. I swallowed hard and gripped Daddy's waist. Looping the lead rope around the horse's nose like a hackamore, he cried, "Let's go, 'Suds!" We bolted off.

"Hey, you two!" Beck shouted after us.

"Hold on, Jess," Daddy commanded.

He didn't have to tell me that.

Soapsuds galloped away. I held tight and shut my eyes.

After a while Daddy sang out, "Whoa, 'Suds! Whoa, boy."

The horse slowed to a walk, then stopped in the road.

I breathed deep and glanced around. "Where are we?"

Daddy looked back, then peered into the darkness ahead. He shrugged. "Don't know. Just outside town I guess."

In the distance I saw flickering lights. Santa Monica? The lights looked like tiny flames. They reminded me of what I'd overheard Beck say in that warehouse and of the awful handbill Leo had found. Of course!

I cried, "Daddy, someone's gonna set a fire tonight in the migrant camp." I quickly told him how I knew. "We've gotta warn them."

"Jess, the sheriff can take care of that."

"Not if he doesn't know about it," I said.

"We can't go riding this horse around like it's ours," Daddy objected. "I've got to take it back to the ranch and get to the sheriff."

"But what about the innocent folks in the camp? What about Leo and his family?"

Daddy twisted around to look at me. Moonlight shone on his face. He started to speak, then hesitated. He seemed to be listening to something.

I listened too. I heard a rumbling sound. Coming from behind us. What—

Beck! He'd turned the car around, and he was headed straight for us. We had to get moving now!

"Hang on, Jess!" Daddy called out.

He kicked Soapsuds into action. We took off down the road. Dark shapes breezed past. Daddy rode well, but I rocked around behind him something awful. I feared I'd fall off to certain injury, so I buried my face in Daddy's shirt and clung to him.

Behind us the lights of Joe Beck's car moved through the trees like a wildfire coming our way.

"Hurry, Daddy!" I shouted.

I glanced back to see the car lights getting closer.

I thought frantically what a horse thief might do if the

horse he'd stolen got away, if a couple of people could identify him to the sheriff. He'd try to run us down, wouldn't he?

Lord, help us escape! I prayed. *Please!*

Ahead, the lights of Santa Monica grew brighter. We were coming into town on some back road. Daddy kicked Soapsuds and yelled to him, *"Come on, boy! Let's go!"*

I could hear Soapsuds breathing. He sounded near winded. We needed more speed. Or another road.

Clutching Daddy tight, I peered over his shoulder. As we rounded a bend, Santa Monica glowed to the left. Suddenly, I recognized this road! I'd ridden it on my bike. And I knew about a trail that led off it. Just on the other side of an old, white, wooden bridge.

I heard Beck's car gaining on us. The car's engine screamed and the trailer rattled a warning.

Then just ahead I spied a white shape in the moonlight. The bridge! *"Daddy!"* I shouted. "There's a trail off to the left! Just past the bridge!"

Did he hear me? I yelled it out again.

"Don't see it!" he hollered back at me.

I didn't dare look back. The roaring car seemed to send out a wave of heat I felt up and down my back. The headlights' beam touched us now. Daddy's shirt lit up before me.

Soapsuds' hooves hit the bridge with a tremendous clatter. It sounded like a whole herd of horses trampling across.

The headlights exposed us and revealed the road ahead.

"Daddy, the trail!" I shouted at him as I spotted the narrow path just ahead.

The car exploded onto the bridge. Beck was about to run us down! My heart thundered.

Daddy abruptly swung Soapsuds to the left. The car tore past, just missing us. We plunged down the trail into darkness. Safe!

Thank You, Lord.

I heard the sound of skidding tires. Daddy reined Soapsuds to a trot. Looking back toward the road, I saw Beck's headlights pointing out sideways, the light filtering through a cloud of dust.

Daddy kept us moving down the trail toward Santa Monica. Before long he reined Soapsuds to a halt not far from the migrant camp.

"The camp's off that way," I told him, pointing to the right.

Swinging around, he said, "You still set on going there?"

I nodded. "There're a lot of poor folks there. Leo and his family too. We've gotta do something to help."

I saw Daddy grin in the moonlight. "You get some of the headstrongest notions of anybody I ever met. We may get in a heap of trouble, but OK. Let's go."

He turned Soapsuds to the right. Nothing but a large, open field separated us from the migrant camp.

In just a few minutes the dark shapes of cars and the flickering of campfires came into view. I saw no sign of any other fire though.

"I don't see nothing unusual," Daddy called back.

"Me neither," I confessed.

We reached the edge of the camp. People sat around campfires. I heard low voices singing and the far-off sound of a guitar.

"Are you sure the fire was supposed to be tonight?" Daddy asked.

"Yes, tonight," I insisted. "I'm sure of it."

Daddy twisted around and looked at me.

"Jess, I've got to get this horse back and get to the sheriff's office," he said. "I've got to tell my side of the story."

I thought of the sheriff. About his determination that Daddy was a no-good horse thief.

"But what if he doesn't believe you?" I asked.

"Don't start worrying now. We'll leave that to the Lord. He's protected us all along, hasn't He?"

I nodded. I knew that to be the truth.

"So, let's get going," he said.

I thought quickly, then made up my mind.

"Daddy, let me off here. I oughta go tell Mama I found you and that you're OK. She'll be worried sick when I'm not home."

He smiled. "You oughta be in bed. That's where you oughta be."

"Please, Daddy. I'll get Mama and bring her to the sheriff's office."

He sighed heavily. "All right, Jess. But you hurry on home, all right?"

I nodded and gave him a big hug. Then I slid down from Soapsuds. I watched Daddy ride away.

I took one last hard look at the migrant camp. Some shadows off to the left caught my eye. What were they? I stared in that direction and picked out two or three separate shapes. They appeared to be men scrambling around in the dark.

Then I saw it. A tiny spark, like a lightning bug except it flared up brighter. Then another, and another. The ground suddenly burst into light at the feet of the shadowy figures.

The fire! It was true. Here were the men intent on burning the camp!

I spun around to look for Daddy. Maybe I could yell for him.

Then I saw another light. A searchlight. Attached to a car, it shot out a harsh, yellow oval. In the center of the oval stood Soapsuds, with Daddy still on his back. I watched as another man stepped into the light. A fat man with a gun leveled at Daddy. The sheriff. Daddy'd been caught! Daddy climbed down from the horse and raised his arms in the air.

I started to run to him. I had to explain what a terrible mistake this was. Tell the sheriff everything I knew. Like—

Suddenly, a sound erupted near the camp. Even before I turned to look, I knew what it was. I'd heard it once, long ago, on our tenant farm in Oklahoma the night that heat lightning struck the dry prairie grass north of our house. That night a southern wind swept the deadly flames just past us to burn everything to the north till they reached a dry creek bed.

The sound of wildfire!

I turned and saw the flames leap. I saw the shadowy men just standing there. The camp still looked calm. No one seemed to notice the quickly spreading disaster.

Behind me I heard a car door slam. The sheriff was carting Daddy off to jail!

I had to help him. But this fire. I had to do something to stop it. Or to warn the people in the camp.

What should I do?

Chapter 16

I decided. I had to warn the folks in the camp. It could mean their very lives.

I turned and whispered, "Forgive me, Daddy." Then I raced for the camp.

At the nearest tent a young couple with a baby sat beside a small, smoky campfire. The man held a battered guitar and softly strummed the strings. The woman's faint voice sang to the baby.

Into this peaceful scene I exploded, shouting, "*Fire!* Quick, clear out! A wildfire's coming this way!"

The man leaped to his feet, dropping the guitar. The mother hugged her baby close and backed away from me.

"Where?" the man demanded, his hands balled into fists, his face frozen with fear.

Pointing at the field, I said, "I saw some men set it."

He ran past me and looked into the field. When he saw the fire, he raced to his wife. "Quick, Helen, take Mary." He looked up, as if checking for the wind. "Thataway!" He pointed in the direction I had come from. "Git as far away as you can. Quick!"

The woman cried, "But Ben, what're you gonna do?"

"Go on, *git!*" Ben shouted.

The woman moved off, slow to leave her husband at first, then running, her baby tight in her arms. The baby's cry erupted in the night like a police siren. Smoke from the fire began drifting into camp.

The man then yanked down his tent and began carrying armloads of battered possessions to his ancient-looking car.

"Girl, go warn the others!" he yelled at me.

Glancing over my shoulder, I saw the fire spreading rapidly. Thick plumes of brown smoke and a bright yellow line of flames rushed across the dry ground.

I ran from tent to tent, crying out, *"Fire! Fire! Clear out!"*

A few folks looked at me in disbelief. But soon the smoke hung thick in the air, burning my eyes. Others now picked up the cry of *"Fire!"* and the alarm spread through the camp.

Men, women, and children ran wildly about. Some of the men pulled down tents. Women carried small children to safety. Some folks just left everything behind and climbed into their vehicles, speeding off into the night.

Then something unexpected happened. Long before I could see it, I heard the low rumble of a car. But not just any car. Along with it came the rattling, thundering sound of a horse trailer.

Joe Beck!

I saw the villain's car tear across the field, the trailer door still hanging down and plowing up the ground behind it. The car headed right for where I'd first seen the shadowy men start the fire.

By now the thick smoke burned my eyes and I started coughing. I thought of the awful dust blows back in Liberal, Kansas. From my overalls pocket I yanked out a bandanna and tied it over my nose and mouth. It helped some.

I hurried back through the camp to where I'd started. There I found Ben sitting behind the steering wheel, trying to get his vehicle's engine going. Possessions lay heaped in the back seat. The engine sounded like an angry, growling animal recorded on a phonograph machine. It growled but it just wouldn't start.

"Mister, you've gotta *hurry!*" I cried out to him.

"I'm tryin', I'm tryin'," he coughed, his face determined. Smoke settled around him, making the scene seem unreal. Ben kept after that engine, trying to start it. I smelled something funny. Not smoke or fire, but something else. What was it—

Gasoline!

"The blamed engine's flooded!" Ben shouted at me. "We gotta get that fire stopped."

"But how?" I asked. I looked at the fire sweeping toward us. Already I felt the heat of the flames.

"If we had us a tractor, we could plow up the ground," Ben yelled. "Make us a trench. That'd stop it."

I felt helpless. We didn't have a tractor. We didn't have *anything!* The camp would soon explode in flames. Some folks would be hurt. Then my mind caught on Ben's words: "make us a trench."

I looked over at Beck's car and the horse trailer, now stopped in the field. Through flickering flames and billowing smoke, I saw the shapes of the fire-starting villains just watching the fire. I spied Beck himself joining the shadowy men.

At that moment I had a crazy idea. Maybe I *could* do something to stop the fire!

Leaving Ben behind, I raced toward Beck's car. My heart pounded. My head ached. A quaking fear shook my body as I ran, dodging flames that licked at my legs.

When I got to the car, I shot a glance at Beck and the men. They hadn't noticed me. Beck had left the car running and the headlights on. I could clearly see the men in the car's lights. As I looked, an awful chill gripped me. My mouth dropped open.

Standing beside Beck was none other than Mr. Hopper. And in his hand I saw a gas can! His face angry, he yelled at Beck, "*You fool!* You let them get away? I told you to hold those kids and to move Land and that blasted horse. Now everything's coming apart! *Fool!*"

Leo had been right. Lex Hopper had double-crossed us. He was a horse thief, just like that dreadful Joe Beck. They had abducted my father. It must've been Hopper who hit Daddy over the head. Anger seized me. I wanted to run over there and—

"*Hey!*" Beck yelled suddenly. Oh, no, he had spotted me. "Hey, you!"

I leaped into the car, slammed the door, then grabbed

on tight to the steering wheel. Could I really do this?

I told myself, *you drove a bit back in Oklahoma, Jessie Land. You can do this. Just ask the Lord to help you.* I said a quick prayer as I pressed in the clutch pedal and pulled down the gear lever. I let out the clutch and the car bounced forward!

Beck and Hopper dived out of the way as the car bumped past them. My only concern now was stopping that fire.

I sat up tall in the seat, but the smoke surging in front of the car worried me. I couldn't see a thing. That and the ruts in the field made the wheel jerk in my hands. I feared the car might jerk right in the thick of those terrible flames.

With all my might I kept tugging the wheel to the left. Slowly, the car eased left. I tromped on the gas pedal and shifted gears. The car burst forward, bouncing over the uneven ground.

I just hoped the hanging trailer door would dig up the ground behind me and make a trench the fire couldn't jump over.

I sped along between the fire and the camp. Then I swung the car around and headed back the way I came. In front of me, through the smoke, I could just make out the path the hanging trailer door had plowed in the ground. It *had* dug up the earth!

I cut a second path, turned around, and went at it again. My second run had drifted a little too far to the right. I tried turning the wheel a little more to the left. The wider the path I cut, the better.

Someone shouted my name, but I kept going, swinging the car around, again and again. It was crazy. A twelve-year-old driving a car pulling a beat-up horse trailer. But I didn't care. I just had to stop the fire.

The flames kept spreading toward me. Soon they blazed only a few feet away. Even in the car I could feel the searing heat. The smoke swept into the car and choked me. Choked me bad, even with the bandanna over my nose and mouth. I coughed so hard I could scarcely breathe. I couldn't go on any longer.

Hopeful the ditch would be wide enough, I took my foot off the gas pedal and stomped on the brake. The car stopped abruptly. I felt a jolt and turned just as the trailer broke free and flew into the fire.

Flames shot up, engulfing the trailer in a fiery embrace.

The fire was on me! It danced at the edges of the ditch.

"Jess, get out!" Daddy's voice called out to me.

I shoved open the door and threw myself out, falling with a thud to the ground. Springing to my feet, I scrambled away from the car and the ditch. The flames swept up on the other side of the car.

The fire stopped at the ditch. But then it fanned out, traveling along the edge. It started to creep around the ends of the torn-up ground.

I'd made the ditch wide enough but not long enough!

Just when I thought all was lost, a miracle happened. The wind shifted.

The fire turned on itself, moving back in the direction it

came from. I watched in amazement as the flames spread out and around the burned area and headed for the group of men in the distance. The men who'd started it all. I heard them shout.

Then I heard another cry from Daddy: "Jess, over here!"

I looked for him and saw him standing beside the sheriff's car, his hands cuffed, his face anxiously turned toward me.

I ran to him and hugged him. The sheriff peeled me away.

Struggling against him, I cried, "Daddy couldn't have stolen Soapsuds. He's been tied up. Look at his wrists. See the rope burns? I can even show you the ropes."

I glanced back at the horse trailer. All that remained was a smoldering husk. The fire had completely burned it up.

And completely burned up my proof—the ropes.

Chapter 17

Turning back to the sheriff, I said with regret, "Well, maybe I don't have the ropes anymore. But just look at Daddy's wrists. He's been tied up. Anyone can see that."

Sheriff Colley replied, "That don't prove nothin'. He could've made those marks hisself. 'Sides, I caught him riding Rogers' horse just a minute ago, sure as shootin'."

"I told you, Sheriff, I was returning the horse," Daddy argued.

I spun around and pointed at the men scurrying from the threatening flames. "You should arrest *them.* Lex Hopper and Joe Beck. *They* stole Soapsuds. They made Daddy write that ransom note."

The sound of a siren pierced the night. The sheriff turned from me and searched the darkness.

"What about *those* men, Sheriff?" I demanded.

"They're comin'," he answered.

I glanced back and saw another man, a deputy I guessed, leading four men toward us. I sighed in relief, but still—how could I prove Daddy's innocence?

As we waited for the men, two firetrucks, their sirens wailing, banged across the field. Fortunately, the wind had died and the fire spread more slowly now.

Hopper, Beck, and the two other men walked up, led by a stony faced deputy. I didn't recognize the other two men.

"This is an *out*rage!" Hopper's voice rang out. "Can't a man look at a fire without being accused of all sorts of blamed things?"

"Settle down," the sheriff said. "I need to find out what you men saw. Anything suspicious?"

The sheriff's words riled me. *"Suspicious?"* I cried. *"He's* the one who set it!"

Hopper glared at me like I was some kind of bug.

I told the sheriff, "You can smell gasoline on him."

The sheriff strode up to Hopper and gave him a sniff. "You *do* smell like gas, Lex."

Suddenly Hopper's anger melted. He glanced at the ground, plunged his hands into his pockets, and began jingling his change. Then he relaxed a bit and smiled.

"Sheriff," he said confidently, "I hate to disappoint you—or this child—but I splashed fuel on my clothes when I gassed up my car tonight."

"That's a bold-faced lie," I announced. The sheriff and Hopper stared at me, Hopper's eyes full of fire. "If he had spilled gasoline on himself, then he's some kind of fool to stand anywhere near a raging fire."

Hopper's mask of confidence faded. When the sheriff turned back to him, he stuttered for an explanation.

At that instant another car drove up. Its headlights flashed in our faces. I heard the vehicle's doors open and close, then the tramp of feet.

A voice sang out: "Gal, you all right?"

Leo!

My friend gaped at me, his black hair going every which way. Beside him stood Frank Dubois. They gazed at the fire, then at the group of us standing with Soapsuds.

Frank began, "I see you got the horse—" But his eyes settled on something. *"Hey, you!* Beck!"

Beck started to back up, but the deputy stopped him.

The sheriff produced a small cornbread muffin from somewhere and popped it into his mouth. "You know him?"

"I'll say I know him," declared Frank. "I fired him four months ago. I thought he'd cleared out of these parts."

As Frank talked in a low voice to the sheriff, Leo ran over to me and Daddy.

"Leo, where've you been?" I asked my friend.

"Perd' near everywhere," he replied, chomping a wad of gum and scratching his wild hair. "I went to the sheriff's, but he was gone. So I headed back to the ranch and found Frank."

In the small sea of light where we all stood, the sheriff announced, "I think you'd better speak up, Frank. This concerns us all."

What now? More lies about Daddy?

Frank cleared his throat and said, "George Land had nothing to do with this horse theft."

What?

He glanced at me with sheepish eyes. "I should've seen from the start. George loves horses. He loves his job. He cares plenty about Mr. Rogers and the ranch. He wouldn't do nothin' like this."

"For pete's sake," cried Lex Hopper. "What kind of investigation is this? He *feels* this way. She *feels* that way. The man got caught riding Rogers' horse! He must've stolen. . . ."

Frank shook his head. "The minute I saw this one here"—he pointed at Beck—"I knew who the real horse thief was. I fired him for stealing. I should've turned him in to the law, but I didn't."

"What'd he steal?" the sheriff asked.

"Some money and this." Frank stretched out his hand. In his palm he held a pocket knife. I stood close enough to read the initials on it: WPR. "It belongs to Mr. Rogers. William Penn Rogers."

Beck's head jerked toward Hopper, then back toward the knife.

"I caught him in Mr. Rogers' house sticking money in his pocket," Frank said. "And this knife too. I made him give the money back and I thought he put the knife down. Later, though, after he was gone, Mr. Rogers asked me if I'd seen his pocket knife about. It'd been a gift from his daddy and he searched the place for it. I knew right then that Beck must have stole it."

"How'd you get the knife back?" the sheriff asked.

Frank glanced at me and replied, "I came upon it in the stable this afternoon. I found a note this girl wrote about a horse. Must've blown off a shelf where she left it. When I picked up the note, I found the knife."

All eyes turned to Beck. He exploded, "So what if you found that crummy knife? It don't prove nothin'. I could've dropped it any time." He stopped himself. Even I saw clearly he'd admitted he stole the knife.

Frank shook his head. "No, you couldn't. You've never been back to the ranch since I fired you. You must've dropped it the night you came and stole Soapsuds."

So Frank hadn't found my note until that afternoon. I asked him, "Why'd you come to our apartment this morning?"

He looked down. "I felt bad about not givin' your mother George's pay. That weren't right. So I stopped by to give her the money. I'd have given it to you, but you ran off."

I frowned. "But what about that quarter horse we borrowed? She ran off—"

"Came right back to the stable," Frank said. "They always do."

Beck stepped away from the group. He shook his finger at Hopper and hissed, "*He's* the one that set it up! He needed the money to pay off debts. He knew when Rogers and his family'd be gone, when they'd be back. He planned it from the start."

Hopper laughed. "Sheriff, that's a downright lie. The cry of desperate man."

Beck yelled, "*You* planned it. I did the dirty work, Lex, but you planned the details. Even had me threaten Land so he'd write that ransom note."

The sheriff's eyes swung back to the merchant. "Lex, you've got some accountin' to do."

Hopper's wild eyes swept all of us. His gaze settled on me. Unexpectedly, he dived forward, grabbed my arm, then clutched me tight in front of him. He backed away.

"Stay where you are," he commanded. "Or she'll get hurt." His arm tugged me fierce against him.

"Ow!" I cried. "Let me loose, you villain!"

"Hopper, let her go," my father demanded.

But Hopper had his own ideas. He backed us up to Soapsuds who stood tied to the door handle of the sheriff's car. He undid the lead rope then boosted me up on the horse's back. He jumped on the car's bumper and then climbed up behind me.

"I'd advise you not to follow," he threatened.

"You harm her, you'll answer to me," Daddy warned.

"It's OK, Daddy," I told him, my voice rattling with fear. "I'll be all right."

"Hopper, you double-crossin' rat," cried Beck. He made a run for us, but Frank caught his arm and threw him to the ground.

"You ain't going nowhere," Frank told him.

But Hopper and I were going somewhere. *Think, Jessie Land, think!* I told myself. I had to get loose of this man.

I could tell by the way that Hopper squirmed behind me that he didn't know horses. Then it came to me. Something I'd seen Mr. Rogers do many times.

I leaned forward and spoke into Soapsuds' ear, "Reach

for the sky, pardner!"

At once the horse reared on his hind legs. His forelegs swung at the stars that hung in the dark sky.

Hopper shouted, *"Hey!"* He pitched backward, crashing to the ground.

Soapsuds danced a bit, then reared again. I held tight to his mane the second time, but the third time up, off I went.

I hit the ground hard. The wind huffed out of me. For a minute I forgot just where I was. When I opened my eyes, Daddy was kneeling beside me, still in handcuffs.

"You all right, Jess?" he asked, his voice urgent.

I smiled at him and sat up, breathing hard. Then I hugged him close and said, "I'm fine now, Daddy."

The sheriff grabbed the still-stunned Hopper. He sent his deputy over to undo Daddy's handcuffs.

"You won't be needing those bracelets now," Sheriff Colley said. "But these two here will, sure as shootin'."

We watched the deputy handcuff Hopper and Beck together, then load them into the backseat of the sheriff's car.

To the other two men, the sheriff warned, "Sam, Pete, you go on home now, you hear? If I ever catch you so much as muttering about migrants again, I'll lock you up faster'n you can say 'pork pie.' " They rushed off and didn't look back.

Frank and Leo worked with Soapsuds to settle him down.

When the horse calmed, Frank said to Daddy, "I hope

you know, George, just what a treasure you've got locked up in that girl there."

Daddy smiled as he lifted me to my feet. "I know, Frank. Her mama and me've known it pretty near since the day she arrived."

Chapter 18

I knew Mama'd be plenty glad to see us. She'd shown strength, what with looking for work to pay the rent and all, but when Daddy and I walked into the apartment that night, her strength left her. She stumbled across the room and collapsed in our arms. She shed a bucketful of happy tears.

Happy as she was, I figure Mr. Rogers was even happier to see Soapsuds again. Frank had taken the horse back to the stable. He didn't really need to tell Mr. Rogers about the trouble. But he did anyway. And I reckon he said I helped get Soapsuds back because Sunday noon Mr. Rogers drove to our place and paid us a visit.

I watched in wonder as the most popular man in America stood in our little living room. Hat in hand, he added a couple of sticks of gum to the gob already in his mouth. He spent a good amount of time gazing at his shoes. He put me in mind of a taller, older Leo.

"Well, um, nice place you got here, folks," he told Mama and Daddy and me. We were just back from church, still in our Sunday best.

He peered at me slyly, chomped his gum, and said,

"Frank done told me how you helped ol' 'Suds." He glanced over to Daddy and said, "Sorry for your trouble in all this, George." Then to Mama, "And for your trouble too, ma'am. The whole thing sounded like more fuss than a convention of bumblebees in a candy factory."

"It all turned out OK," Daddy confessed.

Mr. Rogers handed Daddy an envelope, "Money don't make nothin' right. Fact is, I always thought if you got money you owed it to yourself to get rid of it quick. This's jest a token—for all you done. You and this one here."

He meant me!

Before going, Mr. Rogers made me agree to meet him at an address on Gray Street the next morning. After he left, Daddy opened the envelope. All at once his hands started shaking. Mama gasped, "My land!" That envelope contained hundred dollar bills! With a trembling voice, Daddy counted them. Ten! *One thousand dollars!* I touched one of the bills. Still it didn't seem real. My land!

Come Monday morning I stood on Gray Street at the address Mr. Rogers had given me. It turned out to be Hopper's store! I came close to heading back home. I wanted nothing more to do with Mr. Lex Hopper. But just then Mr. Rogers drove up. He took my hand and we went inside.

"Someone tol' me 'bout a bicycle you've had your eyes on," Mr. Rogers said.

The red bicycle!

I saw his intentions at once, and I smiled at the thought of getting. . . . But then something inside nudged me. I shook my head. "No, sir. You've given my family enough already. More than enough."

"I've seen that contraption your pa strung together an' called a bike," Mr. Rogers remarked. "He did a fine job, Jessie, but I think it's time you might oughta graduate to a store-bought one."

Gazing at the red beauty, I compared it in my mind with the heap of busted bicycle that now lay in the weeds beside our broken down Essex.

"The bike I've got is fine—" I began, but Mr. Rogers would hear none of it.

A man I didn't know greeted us. Everything happened so much like a dream it's hard to remember. Mr. Rogers pointed out the red bicycle and paid for it with cash money.

Outside the store, Mr. Rogers said, "Ol' Lex Hopper's in jail. His trial'll be comin' up pretty soon. You'll have to sit in the witness box and tell what you know. Your pa too. Don't worry 'bout it none, though. A judge ain't nothin' but a kindly father. Most of 'em leastwise. And a jury ain't nothin' but a bunch of snoopy cousins that wanna find out who got theirselves in trouble and how."

"Why did Lex Hopper steal Soapsuds?" I asked him.

He scratched his head and replied, "Way I understand it, ol' Hopper got hisself in a fix with some folks who sold him some stolen goods. I reckon he needed the ransom money to pay those crooks off. He had hisself a whole warehouse fulla loot but couldn't pay for none of it."

Of course, the *warehouse!* Where I'd seen Joe Beck.

Then Mr. Rogers added, "Don't quite know why Hopper was so set on burnin' out that camp. Someone tol' me he blamed Okies for all his troubles. Seems he's the one behind all those anti-Okie handbills and signs. Some folks never quite put the blame for things where it belongs."

He reached out to shake my hand. "I'm goin' back home and ride ol' 'Suds a bit. Might even go take a looksee at that wolf you got tangled up in the trees."

He gave me a wink. Leo must've told him about the wolf—and the bike!

I watched Mr. Rogers drive off. Then I climbed on my new bike.

What a glorious bicycle it was! The pedals worked smoothly and the wheels spun in perfect circles. It was like riding on a cloud. I sped up, then coasted along, testing its smoothness. I think I smiled at pretty near everyone I passed.

After a bit I slowed down, climbed off, and looked over the bicycle. I'd gotten my red beauty after all. My dream bike. So why didn't I feel better about it? Something deep inside gnawed on me. What would God want me to do with this bike? I knew for sure He wouldn't want me to carry on like I was worshiping it. An idea hit me then. A perfectly wonderful idea. But could I carry it out? I didn't know, but I said a brief prayer, asking God for strength. Then I headed straight for the migrant camp.

When I neared the camp, I stopped to stare at the burned grass. Goodness, it had come awful close! I crossed the blackened field and bumped over the trench

I'd cut with the trailer door. Beck's car still sat there, its paint cracked and peeled on one side.

I hopped off the bike and walked it into the camp, looking for Leo.

I heard him before I saw him. He jabbered to a bunch of little kids. It sounded like he had about ten pieces of gum stuffed in his mouth. "Now this here lasso is the one I used over at Mr. Rogers' place to rope me a savage wolf," he boasted. "Quite a trick, lemme tell you."

I pushed the bike beside one of the tents and went up to a woman peeling potatoes. She smiled and said hello.

"Do you happen to know where Leo Little Wolf's family lives?" I asked. They stay around here somewhere."

She gave me a curious look. Then she shook her head. "Leo ain't got no family. He lives here in the camp, all right, but he's on his own. I think he sleeps in Mike MacDonald's car."

"Leo Little Wolf?" I asked, surprised.

She nodded. "A fine boy, but he's got no folks."

Numb, I turned from her and stared at Leo, now in the middle of his yarn about the wolf.

My land, as Mama would say. Here Mr. Rogers gave us a thousand dollars and bought me a bike and the whole time poor Leo didn't even have folks, much less a home, to call his own.

I waved at my friend and yelled, "Hey, Leo, come here."

"Hold your horses, gal," he answered, twirling a lasso to show the kids just how he'd caught that wolf.

My idea had been to give Leo the bike. I wanted to do it. Besides, Daddy could fix up my old one. But now a new idea came to me. Mama and Daddy had said how, with the money Mr. Rogers gave us, we could get our own place. A bigger place. A real home. Maybe they'd be willing to take Leo in. It'd be interesting getting a brother already grown and all. Leo and I could have ourselves some dandy adventures.

And it would be nice to forget about the time folks branded my father a horse thief. Though I guess you could say it was because of a stolen horse that we'd be getting our first real home in California.

ABOUT THE AUTHOR

Jerry Jerman lives in Norman, Oklahoma with his wife Charlene, twin daughters Emily and Hadley, son Andrew, and two cats. He likes Mexican food, baseball, traveling throughout the American Southwest, and really fast roller coasters. When he's not writing about the journeys of Jessie Land, he keeps busy with church and family activities. Now and then he does something crazy like late October sailboat racing in a "frostbite regatta."